GW01185777

AUTUMN

A SURREAL STORIES COLLECTION

DEAN WESLEY SMITH

Autumn

Published by WMG Publishing

Cover design by Stephanie Writt/WMG Publishing

ISBN-13 (trade paperback): 978-1-56146-955-0

ISBN-13 (hardcover): 978-1-56146-956-7

ALSO BY DEAN WESLEY SMITH

COLD POKER GANG

Kill Game

Cold Call

Calling Dead

Bad Beat

Dead Hand

Freezeout

Ace High

Burn Card

Heads Up

Ring Game

Bottom Pair

Case Card

THE POKER BOY UNIVERSE

Poker Boy

The Slots of Saturn: A Poker Boy Novel

They're Back: A Poker Boy Short Novel

Luck Be Ladies: A Poker Boy Collection

Playing a Hunch: A Poker Boy Collection

A Poker Boy Christmas: A Poker Boy Collection

Ghost of a Chance

The Poker Chip: A Ghost of a Chance Novel

The Christmas Gift: A Ghost of a Chance Novel

The Free Meal: A Ghost of a Chance Novel

The Cop Car: A Ghost of a Chance Novella

The Deep Sunset: A Ghost of a Chance Novel

Marble Grant

The First Year: A Marble Grant Novel

Time for Cool Madness: Six Crazy Marble Grant Stories

Pakhet Jones

The Big Tom: A Packet Jones Short Novel

Big Eyes: A Packet Jones Short Novel

THUNDER MOUNTAIN

SEEDERS UNIVERSE

Dust and Kisses: A Seeders Universe Prequel Novel

Against Time

Sector Justice

Morning Song

The High Edge

Star Mist

Star Rain

Star Fall

Starburst

Rescue Two

CONTENTS

AUTUMN

INTRODUCTION

IT ALL MIGHT BE SEASONABLE

For years and years, actually decades and decades, I kept saying that one day I would do a Bryant Street collection or two, and I just never got around to it.

Finally, in the winter of 2023, I decided it was time and told the fine folks at WMG Publishing I was going to do this. Stephanie Writt came up with the cool street-sign logo and I was off.

I thought it would be cool to have Bryant Street be a television series with four seasons of ten episodes each season. (For those of you who don't know, a short story usually has enough story for a single thirty-minute episode of anything on television.)

So I sent the idea of four seasons to Stephanie at WMG and back comes the four wonderful covers using seasons of the year. I was about to object when it dawned on me that four seasons of the year would be a lot easier to explain than four seasons of a television show.

And these would act as ten episodes of a season, but each season would start on the first day of the named season. A full year of Bryant Street.

So I started with the forty stories together and then put them into seasons.

Often a story is set in the title season. Or the story is dark like winter. Or hot like summer.

Or a character in the last days of their lives like winter, or fading like fall. In one way or another, all the stories fit into a season.

But think of them like ten episodes per run. The winter season run, the spring season run, and so on.

Sort of like ten episodes per season of a series like *The Twilight Zone* television series used to be. Every episode different, yet every episode set on Bryant Street.

Smith's
STORIES

Dean Wesley Smith
The Back Seat
A Bryant Street Story

THE BACK SEAT

Andy and Bettie Norwood loved each other beyond doubt. And they loved their old car, an ancient DeSoto.

Then one day Andy got lost on a walk.

And things went from there because, after all, they lived on Bryant Street.

Andy and Bettie Norwood loved their home on Bryant Street. A perfect three-bedroom-down-the-hall ranch with a wooden fence around the backyard and a two-car garage large enough for all of Andy's tools and their only car, a classic two-door DeSoto 1948 Custom Coupe. Andy had bought it used in 1966 right before he and Bettie started dating and he had kept it in perfect shape over all the years.

It was tree green, with the huge steering wheel, no seat

belts, and plastic seat covers that if you took a corner too fast you slid clear to the other side. Just rolling down a window was an exercise routine for either of them. Andy was no longer sure he could still do that.

The thing looked like a giant round tank with tall tires, headlights the size of large platters, and big metal bumpers.

Neither of them drove anymore due to age, bad eyesight, and failing memory. Plus it was work to drive that car. But they loved the car anyway and sometimes they just went out and sat in it, trying to remember the good times of dating and the early years of their marriage.

Both of their kids were conceived in the huge back seat of that car, something they took great joy in telling their children and grandchildren when they stopped by. They both knew they had told the stories of that back seat a hundred times before, but telling them again gave them both pleasure.

And it was fun to watch their kids get embarrassed and the grandkids get appalled. They were old, they had to have a few sports that kept them entertained.

Andy and Bettie also loved to argue. Back when their arguments had fire in them, the making up part also played a large role in those backseat stories.

Now the arguments were just over small things, things that didn't really matter to either of them, and since it was an odd day on the calendar, it was Andy's turn to break up with Bettie.

Someone once asked them why they always pretended to break up and both of them claimed it was not pretend.

But mostly the ritual kept them focused on each other and after all the years they had been together, that was a great thing to give each other.

Andy usually managed to break up with Bettie around two in the afternoon, storm out of the house for a walk, and get back by four in time for a nap and then dinner. The routine got him some exercise as well.

Bettie cooked on the days he left her.

He cooked on the days she got mad and left him.

And the rule of the fights was that nothing was serious enough to call the kids about.

So on a Tuesday afternoon, when Andy slammed the front door and headed off for a walk down Bryant Street, things seemed just fine. He was actually thinking about their upcoming anniversary and the party they were going to have. And that made him happy.

That and the late fall afternoon was beautiful and the trees were pretty in all their colors.

So he just kept walking until one moment he realized he didn't know where he was at.

He had left the subdivision, had turned in a direction he couldn't remember. Bettie always said he was growing more and more forgetful. In fact it had been part of their argument today.

He knew she was right. Hated to admit it, but she was right.

He stopped, looked around.

A busy road with stoplights in both directions. Lots and lots of businesses.

He recognized nothing.

Everything in the modern world changed so fast.

He then just turned around and tried to retrace his steps.

But within minutes he knew he was completely lost.

He had no money on him, no wallet, and no cell phone. All of that was safely on the end table near the door. He had forgotten to grab them on the way out.

And now he was getting tired. He had no idea how far he had walked.

So up ahead there was a small park beside the road, a park that in the dimming light he could not remember ever seeing before, so he sat down on a park bench to rest.

His watch told him that he was now late getting home and Bettie would worry. And he hated worrying her, and she would be mad at him for sure for being such an idiot to get lost in his own neighborhood.

And forget to take his phone and wallet.

And she would be right.

But he had no idea what to do, so he just sat there on the bench, slowly getting colder as the sun went down.

He must have napped for a bit because when he woke up the sun was completely down and he was shivering.

He moved to the edge of the street and just stood there, leaning against a streetlight pole. Maybe Bettie had called their kids and they were out looking for him. He was going to be so embarrassed.

Finally he heard a familiar loud sound. It was the sound of the DeSoto horn.

Bettie was driving and she smiled and waved at him as

she drove by on the busy street and up a half block and pulled into the parking lot of the park and stopped.

If he hadn't been so cold and tired, he might have almost run up the block to meet her. Damn he loved that woman.

She got out and they hugged and then he apologized for getting lost and she just laughed.

She told him she had the heater on and that he should climb into the backseat to warm up.

He asked her why the back seat as she climbed in with him and pulled the door closed and she laughed and said she was lost as well and had no idea how to get home. So there was no point in either of them risking their lives driving.

He agreed to that.

As they sat in the back in the dark, her holding him, him shivering, he realized she had the radio on to an oldies station, soft enough that they could talk but loud enough for them both to hear a lot of the songs that were playing when they first got together back in the 60s.

He asked her if she had called the kids and again she just laughed and hugged him and told him there was time for that. And besides, her purse with her phone was on the front seat.

Then she asked him if he remembered the first time in the back seat that she had taken off her blouse, and as she asked him she started unbuttoning her blouse.

He could see her clearly in the lights from the park and it was as if time had melted away and they were back on the canal road above the orchard and he was with the most beautiful girl in the world.

Time had no meaning.

Making new memories mixed with old was wonderful and after a lot of kissing and laughing and helping each other, the windows on the old DeSoto got fogged up and the old car was rocking when the police car pulled up and a poor young cop shone a light in the window.

Part of the story they told later was how they were both sure the poor young policeman would need years of therapy.

And their son had to pick them up from the police station, totally appalled at their actions, and then walk the ten blocks to get the DeSoto out of the neighborhood park and get it back in the house garage.

The ticket for public lewdness was going to cost them two hundred bucks, and they both thought that totally worth it, but the white-haired older judge they appeared in front of took one look at the description on the ticket, a hard look at them, and then started laughing and dismissed the entire thing.

It seems he understood the magic of a DeSoto back seat as well.

BRYANT STREET

Smith's

STORIES

I'LL SEE YOU

Bryant Street needed a neighborhood watch. But none existed. So Rudy took it on himself to be that watch program, only like anything on Bryant Street, he took it just a touch too far.

No telling on Bryant Street what a person might see.

Bryant Street never had a neighborhood watch program, but if it did, Rudy Edgar would have been its president and major promoter and recruiter. Rudy just wanted to know what was going on around him.

At all times.

Any time of the day or night.

Rudy was rich, single by choice, and liked living in a three-bedroom ranch-style home that looked almost exactly like his parents' home, only slightly more modern. And the neighborhood looked almost identical to his old neighborhood when he was a kid.

He liked watching people back then as well.

He was short at five-three, weighed far too much as far as his doctors were concerned, was bald except for a slight wisp of gray hair on the sides of his head. Every day he got up, went through exactly the same routine, got into one of his silk business suits as if going to work in the old days, and acted as if, during the day, he was at work still. Why not, he figured. He needed the structure and enjoyed it, actually.

He did everything on routine.

He always had, even back when everyone had called him Rudy the Watcher. When the feds turned him into a witness to talk about what he had seen his old bosses doing, he had ended up with a new name, a new identity, and on Bryant Street.

But he still had all his old habits.

Right after he moved in, he had spent a very large amount of money on special spy equipment to watch the neighborhood, much of which was mounted on the highest peak of his house disguised as a set of satellite dishes. Over thirty short- and long-range cameras were up there.

He could watch things for blocks and blocks on his five big screens scattered around his house. He had even done a detailed map of the subdivision. He had it in his spare bedroom on the wall. On it he had labeled each house and kept a file on each house in a massive file cabinet.

Over eighty files.

At first he had used the excuse that he needed to know if his old bosses had found him and were coming after him. After a few years he realized he just liked it.

He knew every resident's car, when they normally left for work or arrived home, and what guests they had over regularly.

He knew who fought, who had money problems, who were happy.

Each file had a lot of information and pictures in them, all carefully dated with carefully typed notes of explanation.

For example, Helen, the woman with the red hair three doors down was having an affair with a guy who drove a green truck with large wheels. The stupid-looking thing often was parked at some spot around the subdivision, as if that didn't stick out.

Rudy had dug into the guy's information and found out his name was Roy, he was married, had three kids, and owed an obscene amount of money on the truck. Of course Helen was married as well, to a man named Craig. Twice Helen had met dear-old-Roy at the door in a negligee that hid nothing. Rudy had gotten some great pictures of her like that.

They were in the file.

She had never met her husband at the door dressed like that. At least not in the five years Rudy had lived on Bryant Street.

In fact, he had pictures of every man, woman, and child who lived in the neighborhood. And it was surprising how many people left windows open on hot summer nights to help him get candid photos.

Every morning at exactly ten in the morning, Rudy made sure his tie was straight, then took a walk around the neighborhood, carrying a notepad and a camera he kept hidden. He nodded politely to anyone who might see him. He knew that he had the reputation around the neighborhood of being the eccentric little man who liked to walk.

After his morning excursion, he went home, had lunch, made notes, and at 2 p.m. he went for another walk with the notepad and camera.

He did it again at 7 p.m. before going home and making himself dinner and watching the neighbors from his televisions.

Rudy liked his life. Was satisfied. He didn't miss his old life much at all anymore.

Until Bettie Jo moved in across the street.

Bettie Jo stood no more than five foot tall, which made her shorter than Rudy. She looked at first to be about his age of sixty-eight, but after he dug into information about her, he learned she was five years younger. She had stunning gray hair that she kept pinned up, but let down at night.

And she seemed to have a light in her eye and a young movement to her step.

She had never been married and had no animals.

At least that was her surface story. Her cover.

Her alias.

Rudy figured out within the first week that the Bettie Jo

look was all fake. He figured she was hiding just as he was. She actually was more like forty and much trimmer than the padding she put on under the Bettie Jo costume.

How did he know all that? Well, there was a tiny slit above her curtains and the angle of his cameras were from high enough that he could see down into parts of her bedroom.

He was stunned at how good she was at putting on the Bettie Jo costume and he started spending more time after his evening walk in his recliner in his living room watching for glimpses of her on his big screen.

He really wanted to talk with her, find out why she was doing so much work to hide. But he didn't dare.

Instead he stayed to his routine exactly, gathering information on everyone in the neighborhood. He knew them all, but none of them were friends. The nature of his life and he didn't actually mind that.

But he was sure he would have enjoyed talking with Helen. She was the most fascinating person on all of Bryant Street.

The routine went on for almost a month.

Then one evening, as Rudy sat in his recliner in his living room, watching for glimpses of Helen, a slight ripple nudged her living room curtain, as if Helen was just on the other side of them.

Something round appeared near the bottom of a side window on her living room. Very small and round.

Rudy sat watching it, trying to figure out exactly what it was when the bullet came though his front window leaving only a small round hole near a lower corner, through his curtains, and smashed into the side of his head.

Rudy the Watcher would never watch another thing.

His past had finally caught up with him.

Late that same night the young version of Helen deftly unlocked the fence gate on Henry's home and then let herself through his locks and into his home without leaving a trace. Henry had trusted the ability to see something coming to protect him more than a decent security system. Helen thought that funny in a pathetic sort of way.

She quickly checked Rudy, but he was clearly dead. Her high-velocity bullet had spread most of the side of his head over the wall and into the kitchen. It would be months, if maybe more than a year before anyone found him. He had no friends and no one ever bothered to check on him.

And even worse for him, he had paid all his bills a year in advance, so not even that would bring anyone looking.

She took some pictures, making sure she got what was left of his face clearly in the shots. She needed the rest of her payday, which was not small, considering that she had been able to finally find and take out Rudy the Watcher.

The little man was the most wanted of all the creeps who turned on the bosses.

Then she carefully went through his place, scrubbing all signs of anything to do with her, planting signs that the house across the street had been empty for months and months.

His map of the neighborhood and all the candid photos of people would be a very good motive for his death.

She fixed the hole in her window the next day without anyone noticing.

One month later a fake investor by the name of James Henry sold the house across the street from Rudy's home to a nice family with three kids. The records showed that the house had been on the market for four months.

It took eight months for someone from the government protection services to finally find Rudy's mummified body.

It seemed no one had really been watching Rudy.

Maybe, just maybe, Bryant Street really did need a neighborhood watch.

Smith's
STORIES

DEAN WESLEY SMITH
USA Today Bestselling Writer

A MENU OF MEMORY

A Bryant Street Short Story

A MENU OF MEMORY

Every day J. C. Dunn comes home to his wonderful house on Bryant Street. He used to love the place, now he fears it. Every night it smells of spaghetti sauce and fresh garlic bread.

He lives by himself and never cooks anything like that. But the smell, every day, persists, like a swarm of insects invading his home.

I wrote this story in honor of my departed good friend Kip. When I started off writing, I worked for him in his spaghetti restaurant. A magical place.

Later on, until he died, he hosted writer workshops that Kris and I taught in his remodeled hotel. I still miss him.

J.C. Dunn unlocked the large wooden front door to his standard ranch house in the subdivision of Bryant Street and just stood there, afraid of what he might find if he pushed that door open.

For years, he had loved to come home to what he called his "retreat in the city." Now, he had come to dread it. The house was starting to drive him slowly crazy.

J.C. was a short man, not more than five-one at best, and he always wore his best suits to work and never took off his jacket. Today was no exception, even though the early fall day was warm and the sun still fairly hot. Normally, once he got inside, he allowed himself to put on comfortable brown cotton slacks, dark brown slippers, and an older dress shirt that he rolled the sleeves up.

He loved that routine. Now he feared it.

He carefully pushed the large door open. The air from the inside hit him squarely in the face. Once again the house smelled of spaghetti sauce. Onion, garlic, green peppers all blended together in a tomato-based mixture. And behind that was the rich, thick smell of fresh garlic bread, like it had just come out of the oven.

The damned smell almost felt hot, it was so real.

Only problem, J.C. Dunn hadn't cooked spaghetti in his thirty years of living in this house. And he had lived here by himself the entire time. And up until just a week ago, the house had smelled normal, like his lilac-scented dryer sheets or the turkey TV dinner he had just heated up. But more often it smelled faintly of old books that he had filled shelves with. And old photos in antique and ornate wood frames he had covered a number of walls with.

He loved that smell, felt comfortable living surrounded by that.

He called all the faces in the old photos his adopted family, even though he didn't know any of them. He had never had a real family, so why not have antique photos of people he could call family.

And often he loved the art of the old carved frames far more than the pictures they contained.

That faint musty odor he loved, but never spaghetti or garlic bread. He wouldn't have a clue how to even start to cook either one.

But for seemingly forever now that garlic and fresh bread smell had invaded his house like a swarm of ants that he couldn't figure out how to kill.

And he had tried.

One day he left all the doors and windows open during the evening. Smell didn't go away in the slightest. He tried air-freshener, but that just created a nasty smell that once again he had to open doors and windows to clear just to get back to the spaghetti smell.

The garlic bread and spaghetti odor didn't seem to be coming from anywhere exactly in the house, yet it was extremely strong and never dissipated. Eating his morning oatmeal over the old-fashioned print newspaper had been ruined. His oatmeal had started tasting like garlic bread, so much so that for the first time in years, he had had to go out for breakfast.

Now his co-workers down at Anderson and Peters Accounting were starting to mention how he smelled like fresh garlic bread. They called it wonderful and said it made them hungry. That has scared him even more because he had almost convinced himself he was imagining the smell.

If others could smell it, it wasn't his imagination.

Something very real was happening and he needed to find out what before he had to leave his wonderful "retreat in the city."

J.C. closed the door behind him and feeling like he was wading through the air, he went and changed clothes. Then he almost swam back to the kitchen to start to cook himself a TV dinner. He had to eat, even if the turkey tasted like garlic.

As he stood there at his Formica kitchen counter, sipping on a glass of white wine, he took out a note pad and tried to write down the first time he smelled spaghetti and garlic bread in the house.

It had been Sunday morning just four days ago.

Four days going on an eternity.

So what had he done Saturday night? Nothing but his normal reading of an antique Zane Gray novel in original hardback with dust jacket.

So what had he done during the day last Saturday? He had had his normal breakfast, then did a little work he had brought home from the office, then made himself a sandwich and put it and a banana in a paper bag and went to the Seventh Street Auction.

He loved auctions, even though he seldom bought anything. He liked being around the people and watching the value of things he remembered as a kid go for stupidly high prices.

And every so often a box of old books would come up for sale and he would bid on them, never going very high. He would maybe keep one or two for his own collection and give the rest away. He was very selective as to what he kept. He was afraid of being a hoarder instead of a collector. He liked his house neat and clean and everything in its place, like a good set of accounting ledgers.

He went to three different auctions a month. It was his one real form of entertainment out of the house.

So what had happened last Saturday at that auction? Now he remembered. He had bought a box of old framed photos. He had put them in his second bedroom until he got a chance to look at them. Could it be one of those framed photos causing the issue?

He didn't see how, but at this point, just short of going completely crazy, he was going to check everything.

He shut off the microwave and let his dinner sit, then headed down the hall to the second bedroom. The house had three bedrooms. His master bedroom, a guest room he kept clean for a guest, which in all the years he had lived here he had never had, and then his third bedroom that he used for his auction hobby.

The door was closed to his third bedroom, as he normally kept it, and inside the small bedroom it smelled the same as the rest of the house.

He had a desk on one wall with a computer on it he

used to look up prices of things on eBay and details about a book or picture he had found.

He had a long folding table against a wall that he used to sort the few things he bought at an auction, deciding what would go to a local charity and what little bit he would keep. He had put the cardboard box of framed photos on the table and hadn't even looked at them since he had been so distracted by the smell.

He had gotten the entire box for ten dollars and the auctioneer said it had come from an estate.

The smell wasn't any worse around the box, but it wasn't any better either.

The first framed picture he took out was of a woman standing beside a horse somewhere on a ranch. It looked to be from around 1920 and she had a nice smile on her face. And the frame almost looked hand-carved and polished. He might keep that one.

The next two pictures were standard family shots of large groups and he set those aside to give away.

The next frame held a menu.

It was printed on what looked like cheap paper and the frame was cheap. The menu was stained with some red sauce, or at least J.C. hoped it was a red sauce and not blood.

The menu was for a place called Kip's Spaghetti Restaurant.

J.C. was stunned. A full spaghetti dinner, plus salad and garlic bread was only 99 cents back then. If he had to guess, it was from the late 1970s or early 1980s.

He looked at the back of the frame. Nothing written there.

He didn't know how it was happening, but he had gotten this framed menu of a spaghetti restaurant on Saturday and starting Sunday his house smelled like a spaghetti restaurant.

Not possible, just not possible.

But neither was a smell hanging around like this. Over the years he had gotten some musty, moldy books that smelled up the house and he had had to take them out and throw them away.

But this was different. Very different.

He held the frame up and looked at it, then decided the best thing to do with it was put it in the trunk of his car to see if that actually helped anything. His logical numbers brain didn't think it would, but he was getting desperate.

J.C. walked the framed menu out to his car, put it in the trunk and went back inside. No one was out in the early evening along the tree-lined street.

By the time he got back inside, the smell had gotten noticeably less, so he opened the windows and doors and within a half hour most of the place smelled almost back to normal. He would have to wash all the sheets and have his suits cleaned and do a ton of loads of washing to get the smell out of everything, but at least he had found the problem.

But he had no idea how an old menu could be so powerful, almost magical in its smell.

He had no idea what to do with it either. No doubt

tomorrow his car would smell like garlic bread, but that, for the moment, was a lot better than his entire house.

That evening he started a few loads of laundry so he would have clean shirts and underwear tomorrow and hung one of his suits out to air on the back porch to get as much of the smell out of it as he could.

The next morning his oatmeal once again tasted like oatmeal and he could just barely smell the garlic bread on his clothes.

But he was right, his car smelled just as his house had smelled for four days.

He opened the car windows all the way around to air it out some, then went back into his house and to his computer after calling work to say he would be in at noon today, something he had never done before.

But he had to do something with the menu, and for some reason he couldn't bring himself to throw it away.

Online he found three different Italian restaurants within easy drive of Bryant Street. He took down their addresses and got in the car, driving with the air conditioning running and the windows open to keep the smell down as much as he could.

The first restaurant hadn't opened yet, so he headed to the next one. There he found the owner after a few knocks on the door. The guy did not invite him in and J.C. was glad for that, to be honest. He had smelled enough Italian food to last a lifetime.

The manager was an older, heavyset guy, about sixty or so, with white hair and large eyebrows. He had to be a ways over six foot tall, so he towered over J.C. but J.C. was used to people doing that.

The guy wore jeans, a too-small T-shirt, and a red-stained apron.

"Hi," J.C. said and introduced himself, standing in the warming sun just in front of the restaurant's door. The owner just stood in the open door and nodded, not bothering to introduce himself. Clearly he expected J.C. to try to sell him something.

"At the auction on Saturday," J.C. said, "I found an old, framed menu of a spaghetti house that I think was around here somewhere."

The manager nodded.

"It's for a place called 'Kip's Spaghetti Restaurant' and it sold spaghetti dinners for only 99 cents."

"You found an old menu from Kip's?" the guy asked, now clearly interested. "My parents and I used to go there all the time. It was magical."

J.C. nodded to that. "I have experienced that. So I am wondering if you would like the menu, no cost. It was in a box of old pictures I bought and I just want to get it to a good home."

Suddenly the big man had a smile on his face that made him look like a kid. "I would love that."

"Let me get it," J.C. said, heading quickly to his car and popping the trunk.

He grabbed the framed menu and handed it to the owner who just beamed looking at it.

"Damn, does this bring back memories. I can almost

smell the place. And the spaghetti sauce was so good and the slice of garlic bread was to die for. I've owned this place for twenty years and I still don't know how Kip did that, let alone sold entire dinners for 99 cents."

"Magic," J.C. said.

"I think it might have been," the manager said, nodding and staring at the menu. He reached out and shook J.C.'s hand, then said, "Thank you."

"I'm just glad it got a good home," J.C. said.

"A great home," the manager said. "Come on in some night. Dinner is on me."

"Thank you," J.C. said. "I just might."

He had no intention of going near this place and that menu again.

Not ever.

J.C. liked his life structured, his books old, and his family made up in antique frames on his wall. He had no time for magic of any sort.

The smell was mostly gone from his car by the time he got to work. And no one said he smelled like garlic bread the entire day.

That night he could actually taste his turkey TV dinner. Life was wonderful on Bryant Street once again.

BRYANT STREET

USA Today Bestselling Writer

DEAN WESLEY SMITH

A Bryant Street Story

IN THE DREAMS OF MANY BODIES

BRYANT STREET

IN THE DREAMS OF MANY BODIES

Harry Stentz killed Cindy Wilson thirty-four years ago.

He even knew exactly where he buried her.

But there, on social media, she appeared with kids and grandkids. And an old picture of herself, the same woman he knew he'd killed.

A twisted short story of a man and a basement on Bryant Street.

Harry Stentz couldn't be looking at the pictures in front of him on his computer.

Those pictures simply couldn't exist.

Cindy Wilson couldn't have kids and grandkids in pictures with her on the internet. She had died thirty-four years before.

He knew that for a fact.

He had killed her.

Yet there she was, smiling at the camera.

Not possible.

He stood up from the computer in his home office and walked into the hallway of his three-bedroom ranch, trying to catch his breath. His slippers shuffled along the hardwood floor as he headed for the kitchen.

He had made a mistake this morning going onto that social media site. He knew better. Now he didn't know what to do.

He had remodeled the kitchen just two years before, putting in state-of-the-art everything. It gleamed and he had kept it shining and clean, even after he cooked a really messy meal. He went to the sink and got a glass of cold water from the tap, then went and sat down at his ornate dining room table.

His kitchen and dining area always had a way of calming him on stressful days.

He had bought the table in case he ever had guests over, but in two years now he hadn't used it for anything but sitting and staring out at his own backyard.

He didn't mind. He loved doing that. The silence was wonderful. It helped him think and plan.

The day was going to be warm and the sprinklers had just shut off, leaving the lawn glistening in the morning sun. He loved green grass and didn't mind paying to keep it green.

He also had his front lawn kept perfectly and the shrubs

and flowerbeds along the front of the house always trimmed and bright with colors. He liked to have his neighbors along Bryant Street know he cared for his home.

And that care cost him a pretty penny every month, but he thought it was worth it.

Besides he worked every day in his home. He wrote novels, detective novels to be exact, all with the same detective. Fifty-two so far and they had made him nice money for thirty-two years now.

So since he worked and lived in the home, why wouldn't he care for it more than anything he had ever cared for in his life. It was his safe place, his work place, where all his secrets lay.

He lived alone.

In fact, he had lived his entire life alone once his parents had died when he was seventeen. And he had lived alone for thirty-five years in this house. He had bought it with his grandmother's inheritance money and figured it would be a perfect home base for him.

Her money had also given him enough time to write his detective series of books.

This house was his entire life.

He finished off the glass of water and stood, moving to put the glass in the dishwasher. Then he reached in under the sink and flipped a small, hidden switch there under the front lip.

He heard a faint click.

He closed the cabinet door and turned and headed into the laundry room just off of the garage. To his right was the door leading into the garage, to his left were the washer and dryer and a shelf for supplies.

Under a storage shelf behind the door into the kitchen was another small hidden switch. He flipped it and heard another small click.

Then he went to the shelf unit beside the washer and dryer and moved one bottle on the top shelf over one inch and then slid the shelf unit forward and to one side.

Behind the shelf unit was a wooden door, the same one that had always been on the stairway down to the unfinished basement since he had moved into the house.

In the first year he had hidden the basement door.

The same year he had killed Cindy Wilson.

He went down the wooden steps carefully, letting the door behind him close and the lights in the basement come up bright.

The place had a damp, moldy smell to it, a smell that made his blood race. He had torn up the concrete floor of the basement years before, leaving only a small area of concrete at the foot of the stairs.

On that small patch of concrete was a large leather recliner, worn with use. He loved to just sit in that recliner and stare out over his life's work.

The rest of the basement was open and ran the entire length of the three-bedroom house.

He stopped and stood at the edge of the dirt, looking out over the entire field of beautiful mounds, carefully shaped.

Each mound was a woman he had killed. Fifteen across

the far wall under his master bedroom and his second bedroom and master bath.

A second row of fifteen closer.

A third row of fifteen even closer.

He was working on the fourth row. Seven of the fifteen possible mounds had been built.

He also had room for a fifth row. He was still fairly young. He had time.

Each mound had an identical wooden box at the head of the mound and nothing more. But the boxes gave that added detail the space needed.

He stepped out onto a well-worn path on the hard dirt between the mounds and moved to the far row and then went to the left to the very first mound in the basement.

Cindy Wilson lay there. He had buried her there.

He picked up the box at the top of the mound and opened it, pulling out a picture of Cindy Wilson and a ring and a bracelet.

It was the same Cindy Wilson he had just seen on the computer. In fact, the very picture he had in his hands had been on her internet page as what she called a "blast from the past."

She had been a long-haired blonde with a bright smile and a biting sense of humor when he had met her. He had asked her out and she had said no.

She had been nice about it, saying she already had a boyfriend, but it was sweet of him to ask.

He killed her two nights later.

She had been beautiful. He tried to kill only beautiful woman, but a few times he had strayed.

He still kept to his routine. Every woman he killed he buried under a mound in his basement, small bits from her life and a picture or two in a wooden box at the head of the mound.

He put the picture of Cindy Wilson back in the wooden box and closed it, then went back to the staircase and upstairs.

What had been online must have been false. That would teach him to never look at a social media site again.

He had known better.

He went to his office and quickly deleted all references to his presence on that site. Then he backed up all his work files twice and stored them.

Then he shut off his computer completely and unplugged it.

Three hours later he was back from the store with a brand new computer. A computer that had not been contaminated with social media and false information.

He spent the entire afternoon setting up his new computer, then headed out to a late dinner.

At dinner in a fine Italian restaurant that smelled wonderfully of garlic bread and red meat sauce, he met a beautiful black-haired woman named Gina. She waited on him and smiled like she really cared.

He found out she was twenty-six, working on saving to open her own restaurant, and was single. She found out he was a writer and really opened up to him.

He remembered every detail, as he always did.

And he even got a picture of her to remind himself of the evening. She hadn't minded at all.

She would be perfect.

Four days later, in chapter three of his new Detective Harry Stentz novel, she died.

In the basement he dug another mound, with another wooden box.

And soon after his fifty-third novel came out to praise and rave reviews, talking about how realistic it all seemed.

Dean Wesley Smith

USA Today Bestselling Writer

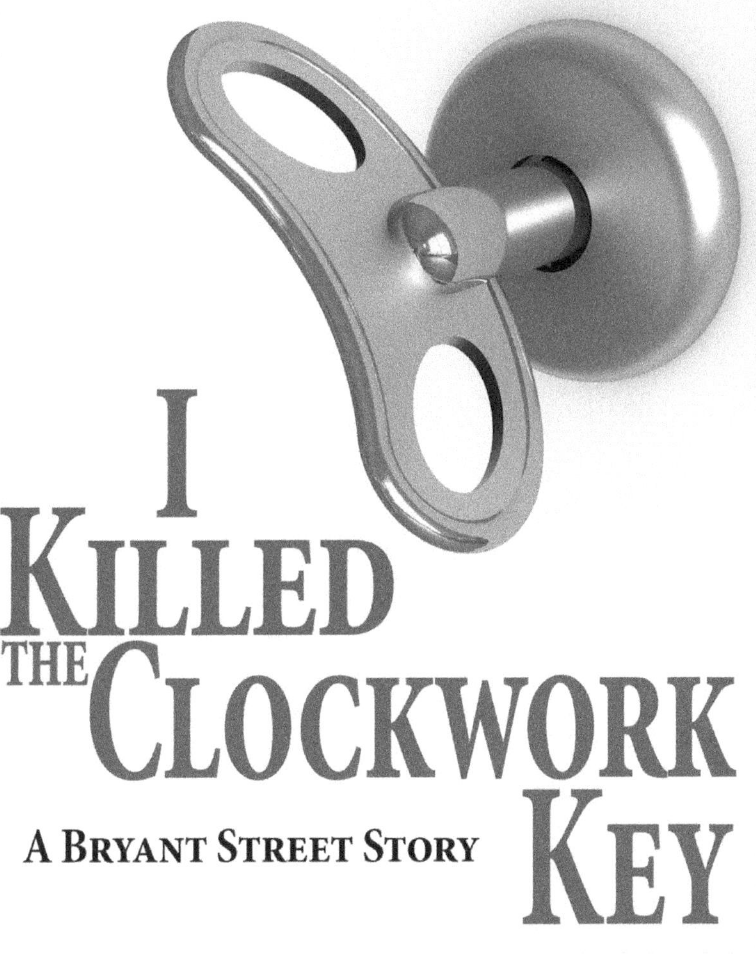

I Killed the Clockwork Key

A Bryant Street Story

I KILLED THE CLOCKWORK KEY

A BRYANT STREET STORY

We are all born and raised with an image of a perfect life, an American Dream illustrated by a simple subdivision street called Bryant Street.

But in chasing and holding the American Dream, we often forget why we are in the race.

For those of you living on Bryant Street, I thought I just might get you wondering why.

The early morning on Bryant Street seemed like any other early spring-morning day in a subdivision that looked like most other middle-class subdivisions in America. Young trees, well-kept green lawns watered by automatic sprinkler systems, clean sidewalks, and a dozen for-sale signs every two blocks.

Half the houses along Bryant Street were bank-owned, and most of the other half had huge mortgages that would never be paid off and would soon also become bank owned.

Barb's and my place was no exception. The Bryant Street subdivision was a small, but beautiful subdivision that might as well be a ghost town.

And I was one of the only remaining ghosts. A ghost of past times on Bryant Street just as any ghost was from a past where life had once existed, but had been killed in a brutal and ugly fashion.

Tuesday had arrived. Monday was finished. The week stretched ahead of me like a dull highway across a flat desert. Or at least I thought it did, until I killed the Clockwork Key, the thing inside of me that wound me up and kept me moving along the same path, in the same circle day after day after day.

We all have Clockwork Keys, but most of us never notice we have them or seem to care.

When I killed my Clockwork Key, I was halfway to my sixty-three-payments-left black Lexus. All normal, until Barb came out of the front door.

"Ram!" she shouted.

She called me Ram because of my days playing football in college where we met. It had been my nickname and she still called me that, even though my real name and the one I liked was Raymond. To her calling me Ram reminded her of better times, better nights of sex and lots of drinking and laughing and throwing parties where kids threw up in garbage cans and behind hedges and called it the "good old days."

I turned, not really caring what she had to say. We had gone through the morning routine. I had kissed her at the door, she had said she thought she was going to have better luck today finding a job. I had told her I thought she would as well.

All simple morning lies to keep us walking along in our circles and not thinking about anything in our life or how we would eventually have to leave Bryant Street and her dream house that we had paid far, far too much to build back when "times were better" as people said.

I'm not sure I remember those times, but people do tell me they existed.

"You forgot your briefcase!" Barb shouted, as if I couldn't hear her in the complete silence of the early morning in a mostly empty subdivision. I was usually the first out of the subdivision these days of the few people that actually left, since I was one of the few on the street who actually pretended to still have a job.

She held up the black briefcase and instead of coming down the sidewalk to bring it to me, she just stood there, waiting for me to come back to her to get it.

And I just stood there waiting for her to bring it to me.

We had a marriage standoff.

Barb and I had had many such standoffs over the years.

But back in the "good old days" or when "times were better," I usually was the one to break the marriage standoff. Now I couldn't care.

I had walked down the sidewalk, I had done my bit to keep the morning moving, to stay in my routine, to continue to pay for the house and the cars and the food for as long as I could, even though we were within six months of being out of money.

She had done her bit to cook the breakfast and to make small talk and to pretend she was preparing to go looking for a job even though we both knew there were no jobs to be had and she would never leave the house or get out of her bathrobe.

We had both played our parts perfectly, just as we did every morning.

Now, standing there on that wide sidewalk with the carefully manicured edges so that the grass wouldn't touch the pavement, neither Barb nor I knew what to do.

We did not know, in our perfectly ordered world, who had the responsibility for the briefcase.

A marriage standoff.

Sure, the black briefcase was supposed to have my job paperwork in it, paperwork I brought home to work on every night, but never did, because I hadn't had a job for over a year.

And in a year of looking, I had found nothing.

And had never told Barb I had lost my job. It just hadn't been worth the problems telling her would have caused me every day. We had long before stopped acting as partners.

And the last thing I had wanted to do was stay in the house with her all day long. I felt bad enough about losing my job and not finding a new one. I didn't need that kind of punishment as well.

My former job was nothing more than crunching numbers to determine who would be laid off next. I assigned numbers, calculations, statistics to people, real people, and then gave those special living numbers to my boss who pretended to check them and then give them to his boss and so on up the corporate ladder until someone decided to act.

Because of my numbers, a certain person or numbers of people each week had been laid off to keep the company profitable (on paper) for the shareholders who continued to send the stock higher and higher making everyone happy who owned the stock.

At first I had felt remorse for the people that my calculations had caused to lose their job. But then, after a few years of doing the same thing every day, every week, I no longer cared about the faces and the lives destroyed behind those simple numbers.

And then one day I had become a number as well. Someone above me had figured the numbers for me and I had been laid off.

Now in our marriage standoff, Barb, once a good-looking woman with brown hair and good teeth, stood there in her blue bathrobe and blue matching slippers on the brown welcome mat in front of our brown and tan home, smiling and holding the worthless lie of a briefcase that contained nothing of value in it.

My life had become nothing of value, either.

It seemed logical I should carry a briefcase that carried nothing.

I stared at her and she smiled at me, holding the briefcase.

And I smiled back and made no movement toward her.

The morning sun felt warm against my back, and I realized that in all the years of mornings I had walked from the house to the car I had never noticed any feeling about anything.

Now I felt warmth.

And the smell of the freshly mowed grass suddenly caught my attention.

And the sounds of birds chirping in the young trees almost distracted me from staring at Barb.

Slowly, her smile faded.

"Ram, don't you need your briefcase?"

I turned my back to her and looked around at the neighborhood.

It was a perfect neighborhood, a perfect, Hollywood-version of a neighborhood, as if some screenwriter had written in a few words at the beginning of a script, "Standard Subdivision: Well-kept and manicured."

I had not really, really stopped and looked at Bryant Street and the homes along the street for a long time. And now that I had stopped, thanks to the marriage standoff, I could actually see what I had missed.

The paint on a few of the empty homes was starting to

show weathering. The shrubs on a few homes hadn't been trimmed in years and had grown too large for the yards.

Windows on two of the closest bank-owned homes were dirty, and the drapes in one window were torn and looked faded.

And as I watched, a woman's face appeared beside the torn curtain, staring at me with sunken eyes and hair that looked like it hadn't been combed in weeks.

A ghost of a former resident, maybe.

I recognized her after a moment. DeAnna Sterling. Or what was left of DeAnna Sterling. She used to be a large, almost obese woman. Now she looked more like a model for a bad fashion designer.

Her husband, Dan had been laid off two years ago and the bank had foreclosed on their home over a year ago.

That home had been DeAnna's dream home, and she and Barb used to be best friends.

I had a vague memory of Barb telling me DeAnna had had a breakdown and had refused to leave her home.

Now I understood why our grocery bill had grown higher. Barb did the shopping, telling me about the inflation. The inflation was that we were feeding DeAnna.

I looked down the street. I wondered how many other ghosts were in these empty buildings and what they did when I was working.

DeAnna ducked back into the darkness of her home.

I turned back to face Barb who had that "worried look" I knew so well on her face. She had not expected a marriage stand-off either this fine morning. More than likely she was missing her morning program and her second cup of coffee, and that was not right.

Or more likely she was worried that I had seen DeAnna.

I stared at my home. I had somehow managed to continue making payments on this "perfect" home. I had started to do the yard work myself when I could no longer afford a gardener, and I drained most of the remains of my estate from my parents to keep walking this routine.

To keep pretending that I was living a life I wanted to live.

I was nothing more than calculations and statistics and numbers as well. My entire life consisted of walking the same routine, doing the same thing, trying to find a job that didn't exist to pay bills I didn't want to pay so that I could keep doing the same thing again and again and again.

And now, because of a briefcase and a marriage stand-off, I could see clearly for the first time what I had been doing.

I had broken the cycle.

I had broken my Clockwork Key.

I reached up and undid my tie because I was getting warm standing there on the sidewalk in my black suit.

Barb's "worry look" switched to her "puzzlement look" mixed with her "slight-panic look." I knew all her expressions. I knew how she thought at every moment of every day.

I dropped my tie on the grass I had mowed yesterday after I had gotten home from my pretend job.

"You keep the briefcase," I said to Barb.

"Ram!" she shouted, her voice rising to the level I hated, the level that made her sound like a record had spun up just a little too fast while she spoke. "What are you doing?"

"You keep it all," I said, waving at the home I had come to hate and the neighborhood I had never really looked at in years.

"Ram? What's wrong?"

She had still not moved off the porch, and was now clutching my briefcase against her chest as a symbol of the life she didn't want to lose. An empty briefcase that meant far more to her than I ever did.

"Nothing's wrong," I said, smiling at her. "I've got to go. You keep it. You keep it all. You win."

With that I turned and walked the short distance to my car and got in.

She still stood there in front of the worthless home, in her blue bathrobe with perfectly matching blue slippers, my empty briefcase clutched against her chest.

I still had enough savings left to get a divorce, give her the house in the settlement, pay off my car, get a nice, cheap apartment in some other town where there were still a few jobs to be had, and maybe eat for a year or more.

After all, I was a numbers man and I knew the numbers. I had lived those numbers for years now, walking in clock-like service to a life I did not want with a woman I had grown to hate.

I pulled out of the driveway and stopped in the middle of Bryant Street, giving it one more look.

Barb clutched my briefcase, staring at me.

I smiled at her, a real smile for the first time in years. Not a pretend smile, but a smile I actually felt.

I waved at her. Then, with my hand solidly planted on the horn, I drove down Bryant Street for one last time, letting the loud sound of my leaving echo off the ghost-like remains of my former life.

BRYANT STREET

Dean Wesley Smith

USA Today Bestselling Writer

A Life in Whoopees

Great Moments Exist For All of Us

A LIFE IN WHOOPEES

Great moments exist for all of us at different times in our lives. From a simple taste of a cookie to meeting the love of our life.

Bill Wallace lived through five of those special moments. Bill considers himself lucky to experience five. Many people never get any.

A LIFE IN WHOOPEES

My name is Bill Wallace, I'm seventy-two years old, and I feel like one of the lucky people in life. I had a good marriage, great children and grandchildren, a good career. And I had five whoopee moments.

I hear some people never even have one.

MY FIRST WHOOP

I was ten. It was the last day of school before Christmas, and it was snowing lightly outside our family house in Madison, Wisconsin. As I came through the door, the warmth of the house hit me in the face, combined with the fantastic smell of Mom baking Christmas cookies.

"Yes!" I shouted. I dropped my backpack on the hall table and headed toward the kitchen.

"Billy!" my mom shouted from the kitchen. "Take off your boots at the door."

I stopped, yanked off my boots and went sliding in my stocking feet on the hardwood floors to get a cookie.

That Christmas turned out to be the best Christmas ever, since Grandma and Grandpa were there, Dad was still living at home, and Mom seemed happy. None of that would ever happen again, so I still look back at that Christmas as the best ever.

MY SECOND WHOOP

Debbie pushed me away and slid back across the front seat of the car. She was clearly breathing hard and as excited as I was.

We had parked on a canal road a good four miles outside of town. The only thing close was a farmer's house a half mile away. I still had the car radio on, and the light from it and the moon through the steamed-up windows was enough for me to see Debbie's face.

Her short brown hair was messed up slightly, and her cheeks were red.

Debbie and I were both sophomores in high school and had been sort of hanging out for a month or so together. It was common knowledge that we were together, and we went out on sort-of dates a lot, but that was about as far as it had gotten.

Twice after I had gotten my driver's license, we had parked out here on the canal bank, and both times all we had done was kissed. I was hoping tonight might be a little different, but so far it was turning out to be the same.

The seat between us was one of those bench seats that only Dodges and pick-up trucks had during the seventies. Luckily my mom had bought a Dodge.

"Billy, you promise you won't tell anyone we're parking?"

"Who am I going to tell?" I asked. "Of course I promise. What happens here, what we talk about here, is just between you and me."

She looked at me for a long time, but of course, in that situation, any amount of time seemed long. Then, in a quick motion, she slipped her sweater over her head and tossed it into the back seat.

Her white bra was like a beacon in the night. All I could say was "Wow!"

Five years later, during our second years in college, we were married. I have to admit that even after we were married the sight of her in a bra still took my breath away.

MY THIRD WHOOP

The letter came from the State Bar association. Four years of college and three years of law school and it all came down to one stupid envelope in my hand.

I just stood there in the doorway of our apartment, staring at the envelope. I couldn't stop my hand from shaking.

Debbie, who had spent seven years putting me through college, looked at what I was holding, then gently took it out of my hand.

I was already an associate at *David, David, and Jennings*, one of the best law firms in town. But I still had to pass the bar, and the results of that bar exam were inside the envelope. Three weeks ago I had walked out of the exam convinced I had passed, but with every day since I became less and less sure, to the point where I could hardly sleep I was worrying about it so much.

I couldn't watch as Debbie quickly opened the letter.

Then, in the loudest release of breath I had ever heard, she handed me the letter and then hugged me, smiling and crying at the same time.

I glanced at the letter. I had passed.

"Oh, thank God!" I said.

"You did it," Debbie said.

I looked her right in the eye and shook my head. "We did it."

All both of us could do after that was just smile.

MY FOURTH WHOOP

My secretary knew what I liked. We'd been having an affair for almost a year, and she said that she had something very special for me for Christmas this year.

Debbie and I had had two kids, a boy named Ben and a daughter named Karen. With Debbie focusing on the kids and me focusing on building my law practice, we sort of drifted apart. At some point a few years back we just sort of stopped making love, one or the other of us seeming to always be too busy. We talked about it once in a while, but never really acted on the talk.

We also fought a lot, especially right after the kids were born. It seemed I never knew when I went home if Debbie was going to be angry or not.

I don't think Debbie knew I was having an affair with my secretary, Heather, and I never wanted her to find out. She had developed a real temper over the years, and I sure didn't want her letting that temper loose on me for something as major as an affair. It was bad enough on the small stuff with the kids and the house and money.

Heather knew I was never going to leave Debbie, and she didn't much care. She was open sexually and had no thoughts at all of wanting me as a husband.

"So what's this surprise you've been talking about?" I asked Heather as I came back into my office after my last meeting. It was a little after six in the evening three days before Christmas, and Debbie didn't expect me home for at least another few hours.

Heather beamed at me, her twenty-something smile lighting up the room. She had long blonde hair, even longer legs, and a body that looked far too good in a lace bra and underwear.

"This way," she said, motioning me with a finger.

She had that sexy look on her face and I knew I was in for something fun.

She led me into my darkened office, and then before I could turn on the light, she put her hand on mine and said, "Not yet. I'll tell you when."

She closed the door and turned the lock, sending the room into almost complete blackness, since the blinds were down on the window and it was a dark night outside.

I could hear a faint rustling in the dark. Then Heather said, "Go ahead."

I snapped on the light. The sight that greeted me was something I could have only dreamed about. Heather and another young woman were both sitting on the edge of my desk. Both were wearing only lace underwear. The sight took my breath away, so it was a moment before I finally said, "Wow!"

Heather smiled at me. "This is Heidi, a friend of mine. She's going to help me give you a very special Christmas present."

Two and a half hours later I finally managed to stagger to my car. Never, in all my life, had a Christmas been like this one.

MY FIFTH AND FINAL WHOOP

I was just over an hour late getting home after my special present from Heidi and her friend. I expected to find Debbie sitting in her favorite chair, watching television, wrapped in her blue bathrobe, more than likely angry at me. But instead, when I opened the door, I was greeted with the wonderful smell of baking cookies.

I took off my coat and dropped my briefcase on the hall table, then headed for the kitchen. I had skipped dinner because of Heather's little surprise, so the smell of the cookies was almost more than my rumbling stomach could handle.

When I went through the kitchen door, I got a sight that not in a million years would I have expected to see. Debbie was leaning over the stove in her white lace bra and underwear, taking out a fresh batch of cookies.

Until that moment I hadn't realized just how attractive she still was. Even after having two children, she had kept herself fit.

"Wow!" I said, for the second time in the same night.

She looked up at me and smiled. "Welcome home. I thought I'd give you a little surprise."

I glanced around, then back at her. "Where are the kids?"

"At my mother's for the night," Debbie said, smiling her old sexy smile. "So we're all alone."

She put the hot batch of cookies on the stovetop, closed the oven, and moved over to a plate of cookies already frosted. "I bet you're hungry," she said, offering the plate to me.

"I am," I said, taking two cookies. "And these smell wonderful. And you look wonderful."

I almost swallowed the first cookie whole, it tasted so good.

"I do, don't I?" she asked, turning around so that I could see her from all sides.

"You do," I agreed between bites of the second cookie. "Really good."

"As good as Heather and her friend Heidi?"

I froze in mid-bite, staring at her smile.

She laughed, twirling around to give me another look. "I'm surprised you would even be interested after what those two young things put you through in your office."

I had no idea what was happening, how she knew about Heather and what had happened in my office, or how she was even going to react. So being a good attorney and a fearful husband, I ventured nothing, and said nothing.

She leaned against the counter across the kitchen from me, that damned white lace bra of hers making her look very sexy. "Surprised, huh?"

I nodded slightly and she laughed.

It was getting damned hot in that kitchen at that moment. Too hot.

"Didn't you know I would find out what you were doing? Hell, I went to take you to dinner to talk about things and even got a little show tonight."

Damn, she had a key to my office. I had made her one years ago.

"So I thought I'd just come home and give you a little show of my own."

I could feel my heart racing, my blood pounding through my head. I couldn't seem to think straight.

I tried to say something, but the words didn't want to come out.

"Oh, good," Debbie said, laughing and coming toward me, "the poison is working."

I wanted to say, "Cookies?" but again nothing came out.

The next instant, instead of staring at Debbie's white bra, I was watching the tile Debbie and I had picked out specially for the kitchen come rushing up at my face.

I woke up six hours later in the hospital. A woman who looked like a doctor was standing over me, frowning.

"Poison," I managed to croak out.

"We know," she said, nodding and staring at some instrument beside me. Then she patted my arm. "Just rest."

I must have rested, because the next thing I remembered was waking up to the blinding light from the window, my head pounding so hard I thought it might explode.

Debbie was already in jail. She served a total of six years in prison for trying to kill me.

I lost my position in the firm and had to hang out my own shingle because it came out in court what Heather and I were doing that caused Debbie to snap.

The kids lived with me, with my parents helping out, and visited their mother every other Sunday while she was in jail, and every other week after she got out and got a job. I never did make as much money as I had been making at the firm, but I did all right for myself over the years. And never once hired a secretary.

I never remarried either. Couldn't see much point in it.

I was thirty-two when Debbie poisoned me with that cookie. Now I'm seventy-two, no longer practice law, and have three wonderful grandkids. But in all those years, I never had another whoopee moment.

I guess I should be happy to have a five-whoopee life.

From what I understand, some people never even have one.

I feel sad for them.

BRYANT STREET

USA Today Bestselling Writer

DEAN WESLEY SMITH

A STUDY OF AN ACCIDENT

A Bryant Street Story

A STUDY OF AN ACCIDENT

Dan remembers clearly the time before the accident.

He remembers his wonderful wife and daughter. Impossible to forget. He refuses to eat or work or even move most days.

He made a mistake, they died. He lives. He blames himself for their deaths.

Someone knocks on his home door. And the truth flips as only it can on Bryant Street.

ONE

The blinds of the living room had been closed for six months, and only two light bulbs still worked, giving the room a constant feel of depressive gloom. Deep black shadows extended from the once-modern furniture, extending across the oak-colored hardwood floors like stains.

The room smelled of rotted food, a foul odor that now seemed to have gotten coated onto everything.

The television flickered, casting its own light and then dark shadows around the room as scene after scene of meaningless programs and ads ran past.

Six months ago, this house had been alive, a bright place to live and raise a family.

Dan and Jennifer and ten-year-old Denise had all been happy together.

Sitting in his chair in the dark living room facing the mindless television, Dan could imagine he sometimes still heard the happy laughter of Denise as she played in her room down the hall or helped Jennifer with dinner or a project.

Denise, with her bright smile, blue eyes, and long blonde hair used to light up a room wherever she went. Her mother, Jennifer, had been the same way.

And often the three of them would watch a movie together, Dan in his chair, Jennifer and Denise on the couch, a bowl of popcorn between them.

He had loved those movie nights.

Magic nights he would tell Jennifer later, after Denise was off in her room.

And Jennifer had always agreed.

Now the house was dead.

He might as well be.

It had been an accident.

TWO

The day of the accident started like any normal Tuesday. He kissed Jennifer goodbye in their kitchen and then gave Denise a squeeze and a kiss.

He got into his BMW to head to his office in the McClaskel building. He worked there as a corporate attorney, specializing in property acquisitions.

He liked his job, actually. Found it interesting and challenging and rewarding since he and Jennifer never really were short of money.

He also liked his new car and the new-car smell of the leather. He splurged and got himself a new BMW every year, mostly because he could.

His office was a corner office on the sixteenth floor looking over the downtown area of the city. He had two large plants that framed the windows and a large mahogany desk, plus a couch and chair tucked against one wall with a mahogany coffee table in front of them.

It was a beautiful office.

He hadn't returned to it since the accident.

They were holding his job for him, but he wasn't sure if he could ever return.

On the day of the accident, everything had gone normally. He had had lunch with two of the other lawyers and three assistants in a nearby pub. He even had a glass of freshly brewed ale. He remembered it tasting smooth and rich and he planned on returning the next day for another glass.

He wasn't much of a drinker, but he enjoyed a good ale.

Back in the office after lunch, he had worked on two cases, one right after another and by three p.m. he had finished up both.

That was when Anna from accounting came in and asked him for some of his time to figure out a few things about a third case. She had an accounting puzzle she needed his help with.

Now Dan had flirted with Anna a few times, but all innocently. He had never fooled around on Jennifer and had no thoughts of doing so.

He loved his wife and his daughter more than anything in the world.

Anna was about his age of thirty-five, had long blonde hair, and large green eyes. She also had a bright sense of humor and a body that looked like it was out of a swimsuit issue of *Sports Illustrated*.

He had heard she was divorced with no kids and was enjoying her freedom, but he didn't ask her about any of that.

The day of the accident, Anna had on a white blouse that showed hints of a lacy bra under it. She had on a business skirt and had her hair pulled back and tied.

For over an hour, they sat on his couch, side-by-side, going over the accounting ledgers she had brought on the coffee table. They joked and laughed and he enjoyed the company and the challenge of finding what they were looking for.

By 4 p.m. they had finished and were both sitting on the couch sipping on bottles of water, just talking.

And then something happened that surprised Dan and made him feel really powerful at the same time.

Anna leaned over and kissed him.

Her kiss was very different from Jennifer's tentative butterfly kiss. And as Anna kissed him, she pressed into him and he responded, kissing her back.

And the next thing he knew, he had tipped over on the couch and she was on top of him.

They were both still dressed when the first part of the accident happened.

"Daddy! Look what I bought!"

His office door opened and in walked Jennifer and Denise, both smiling until they saw the scene on the couch.

They both stopped and stared.

Anna scrambled to her feet, grabbed the accounting ledgers from the coffee table and fled while Dan just stood there.

He didn't know what to say to either his wife or his young daughter.

What could he say?

After a moment, Jennifer had said to him in her cold, angry voice, "We need to talk when you get home."

He had nodded.

Jennifer took Denise's hand and they turned and left without another word.

That was the last time he had seen them.

By the time he had managed to collect himself to go

home and explain to Jennifer what had happened, the second part of the accident had happened and his wife and daughter were both gone.

Dead.

Fifteen minutes after leaving his office, Jennifer had drifted into the oncoming lane of traffic and was hit by a large semi-truck.

Both Jennifer and Denise were killed on impact.

Dan knew he had killed them because Jennifer must have been crying while driving and she had never been that good a driver as it was.

He had no memory of the funeral.

He had little memory of the last six months sitting in his dark empty house.

He was as good as dead as well.

He just hadn't stopped breathing yet.

THREE

At some point on some day around six months after the accident, there was a pounding on the door.

Dan assumed it was in the middle of the afternoon because of the program flickering in front of him. But he wouldn't have bet on even that much.

"Go away," he shouted from his chair. "I'm not buying."

"It's Detective Carson," a man's voice shouted back. "I need to talk with you."

Dan just shook his head, clicked off the television, and climbed to his feet. He had on jeans that hadn't been washed in any recent memory and an old work shirt he had put on a few days ago as one of his last clean shirts left.

He went to the front door and opened it, letting in the bright light that made his eyes hurt for a moment. Clearly it was a nice day outside.

The quiet suburban street he lived on seemed extra quiet at the moment. Only a black sedan seemed out of place along the green grass and flowerbeds that lined the street.

A heavy-set man stood at the door holding his gold badge. "I'm Detective Carson. We have the results of the cause of your wife's accident."

Dan just shook his head and stepped out on the porch to talk with the detective.

Carson had a strong grip and seemed to give off an air of control. He was fairly short and had a large beer-gut pushing out his suit coat.

"They are dead," Dan said. "Car accident ruled Jennifer's fault. Why investigate?"

"We have to do a complete investigation on all fatal accidents to determine the exact cause."

"And did you?" Dan asked, not really wanting to be a part of this conversation.

"The cause of your wife and daughter's death was because she was distracted while driving," Carson said.

Dan knew that.

He knew he had been at fault. He didn't need to have some detective tell him that.

Dan knew that he had killed his wife and daughter.

Then Detective Carson said, "She was texting."

That shocked Dan to his core.

He blinked twice and looked at the detective, who was just staring at him.

"Texting?" Dan asked, making sure what he had heard was correct.

The detective nodded. "Were you and your wife having marriage issues?"

Dan opened his mouth, then closed it. Then managed to ask, "Why?"

"This is her final text," Carson said. He opened a green file he had been holding under his arm and handed Dan a sheet of paper.

The words made no sense at first and it took Dan twice reading them before he actually understood what they said.

I am free!!! Caught bastard with your friend. Divorce to follow.

There was a response.

"Wonderful! We can finally be together. I knew Anna would come through!"

When Dan looked up from the page, Detective Carson said, "She was texting her response when she drifted in front of the truck. Do you know who she was texting to?"

"Do you?" Dan asked, reading the words one more time and trying to get them to sink in.

He had been set up. Jennifer had wanted to leave him. But because of Denise, she couldn't. So Jennifer had set him up with Anna.

There would have been no way after that for him to argue against a divorce.

"I do," Detective Carson said. "Do you know a Susan Fields?"

"Jennifer's best friend," Dan said.

Dan remembered her standing off to one side at the funeral, crying. She was being comforted by another woman and an older man. Dan hadn't been up for talking with her.

"Very, very best friend," Carson said. "We dug up evidence that Jennifer and Susan had been having an affair for years. Since right after your daughter was born, it seems."

"Oh," Dan said, more stunned than he had felt since hearing the news of Jennifer and Denise's deaths.

Jennifer was gay and having an affair.

None of that made any sense at all in the wonderful life the three of them seemed to have had.

"You didn't know, did you?" Carson asked.

Dan shook his head.

"I didn't think so," Carson said.

"Does Susan know she was the one that killed Jennifer and Denise?" Dan asked.

"She did," Carson said, nodding. "She overdosed a month after the accident."

"Oh," was all Dan could say to that as well. Susan wasn't even around to be angry at and blame.

But Susan had had more courage than he had had over the last six months. He had just wallowed in self-pity; she had acted on her grief.

"Here is a copy of the file on everything we discovered

in the investigation," Detective Carson said. "I figured you needed to know."

Carson handed him the thin file.

"Thank you," Dan said.

"There is one more thing I think you need to know as well," Carson said, standing there, looking like he might jump and run. He didn't look happy at all telling Dan all this and Dan didn't blame him in the slightest.

"Worse than this?" Dan asked, holding up the file.

Carson nodded. "The information is in there, but figured it was better to hear it coming from me than just read it."

"Go ahead," Dan said.

"Denise was not your biological daughter," Carson said. "We did mandatory DNA matching after the accident and discovered that fact fairly quickly. We have no idea who the father might have been."

Dan nodded, holding onto the folder like it was about to burn him.

Actually, the news in it had already burned him.

And oddly enough, the same news gave him a flickering flame of life again.

"Thank you, Detective," Dan said. "I mean that."

"If you need my help on anything," Carson said, "feel free to call."

Dan nodded and stood in the sun on his front porch, holding the folder with his past and his future in it as Detective Carson walked back to his black sedan parked at the curb.

Then Dan turned and went back into the darkness of his home.

In one conversation, it had become his home now.

Not the burial chamber for every member of a supposedly happy family.

Jennifer had wanted to leave this house and take Denise.

And she must have known that Denise was not his child.

Dan wondered when she was going to tell him that bit of news. More than likely after a lot of years of child support.

But that didn't matter. He would have always thought of Denise as his daughter, no matter what.

Jennifer and her lover Susan had taken Denise from him.

He would never forgive either of them for that.

Ever.

He put the folder in his chair and went to the blinds and opened them on all the front windows.

And then he opened the windows as well, letting in the fresh air of a new day.

There was a lot of smell to get out of this house.

Smell of stale food and dirty laundry.

Smell of six months of self-pity.

And the smell of years of betrayal.

But the bright light of the truth and a few open windows to a future might just be what was needed.

USA Today Bestselling Writer

DEAN WESLEY SMITH

THROUGH THE FOR SALE SIGN

A Bryant Street Story

BRYANT STREET

THROUGH THE FOR SALE SIGN

Strange things always happen on Bryant Street.

Unexplainable things. George Wayne Hooper loves living there.

Former real estate agent, George's talent for reading houses fits the weirdness of Bryant Street.

Another twisted tale of the strange life on the normal-looking Bryant Street.

George Wayne Hooper stood on the sidewalk staring at the For Sale sign that had just appeared that morning in the dry weeds of what used to be the front lawn of Dot and Dan's home. It had only been a matter of time before the sign would appear. He knew that. Bank notices had been on the door for months.

Today it seemed the house might start to find a new owner. Finally.

Around him the dry air of a Boise fall day was promising to be warm, even though the morning air still had a bite to it. He looked both ways along Bryant Street, the long suburban street turning slightly to the right about seven houses away.

Except for Dot and Dan's traditional three-bedroom ranch house, all the other homes along Bryant Street were well maintained, including his own about twenty houses to the left.

George loved his morning walks after everyone else had left for their regular work. Exactly two miles long, he circled the entire subdivision and walked past every house seven days a week.

He had done that for years since his wife Madge had died, so he knew just about everything that happened on this street. He never talked to anyone about any of it, but he enjoyed knowing.

Very few children lived along Bryant Street and almost always both partners in a home worked. He was the only retired person who lived alone on the street. So he always felt every weekday morning he had the entire subdivision to himself.

Today was Tuesday and no one was home anywhere in sight. The air was still with no wind and the only sounds were some birds around a feeder two houses away and the rumbling of traffic in the distance from the unseen freeway.

George stood not more than five-two with his dress

shoes on. But since Madge had died, he never wore any kind of dress clothes. Had no reason to. Mostly he just wore his tan slacks, a tan dress shirt covered by a brown button-down sweater, and tennis shoes.

He and Madge had no children, and at seventy, most of his friends were dead or in homes dying of one thing or another. He figured his morning walks had helped keep him healthy.

When he did happen to run into someone on a weekend, he always smiled and waved and they always smiled and waved back. He was like a light post or a street sign in this subdivision. He was just part of the place, a part that no one noticed unless forced.

And since he made no trouble and made no one actually look at him and ask questions, he got to do what he wanted.

And he honestly liked it that way, especially on mornings like this.

Today, he would finally get a chance to see what exactly happened to Dot and Dan. One day this light-brown home had been just another home he walked past, the next they were gone and the place had been emptied out.

He never saw a moving truck or any packing activity at all. And he hadn't missed a day on his walk.

Very strange.

On Bryant Street, a lot of strange things happened with frightening regularity, but this was one of the strangest.

He had been waiting patiently for the For Sale sign to go up. Now it was here and today was the day, finally, he would get some answers.

Before he retired to take care of Madge as she had been eaten by cancer, he had worked as a real estate agent. He had done it his entire life and he was stunningly good at it, making himself and Madge very rich.

He had discovered when he started into real estate that he had a special talent he never mentioned to anyone, including Madge.

By simply touching a For Sale sign and then going inside the house and touching something in the house, he knew everything about the previous tenants. All of them all the way back to when the building was built.

He had ignored that talent at first, thinking he was going crazy. But the more he researched what he just "knew," the more he came to trust it.

And he decided early on he would never hide anything about a house from any potential buyer. And by being honest with the buyers, he quickly made a reputation for himself as the person to go to when someone wanted to buy a house.

But now, retired, his skill was only for times like this, when his curiosity really wanted to find out what happened in a home.

He looked both ways and then started up the home's sidewalk through the weeds of the front lawn and planter beds.

A realtor lock-box hung on the door as he expected it would. He had kept his real estate license up so he could legally enter the home without getting into any problem.

He took out his cell phone and called the listing agent,

identifying himself and saying he wanted to take a quick look at the home on Bryant Street for a client.

The listing agent gave him the lock box combination and he was all set.

He went back to the edge of the street and touched the For Sale sign, then moved up the sidewalk again, trying to walk slowly even though the excitement of the moment was more than he had felt in a year.

He opened the lock box, got the house key and unlocked the front door. He put the key back in the lock box and closed it before stepping inside and closing the front door behind him.

With the slight thump of the door shutting, he had vanished from his morning walk.

The house smelled musty as he had expected it would from being closed up and empty for so long. The blinds were all pulled and the inside was empty and dark.

So what had happened to Dot and Dan? He had never met them, but they had looked so normal the numbers of times he saw them. Both had been in their early thirties or so. Both attractive. No children, but seemingly a lot of friends.

George clicked on the lights in the carpeted living room area.

No furniture remained.

Nothing.

Just an empty expanse of light-blue carpet that showed some stains and a lot of dirt around the ends. A kitchen and dining area was beyond an archway toward the back of the house and a hallway led off to the right to the three bedrooms and two baths.

It was at the moment that he touched the light switch that he knew what had happened to Dot and Dan.

His knees got weak and he had to hold himself up against the wall near the front door.

Dot and Dan had been the third owners of this home. One couple by the name of Swenson had originally built the house and sold it four years later to the Craigs. They had sold it to Dot and Dan five years ago.

And from what George could tell from his vision of previous owners, Dot and Dan had been happy here until one night eight months ago.

It seems Dan had been a jeweler by trade.

George kept his hand pressed against the wall not only for support, but to keep the information flowing from the house to him through his special power. He made himself take deep breaths of the musty air, trying to calm his nerves.

It also seemed that Dan and Dot had been doing a little import business on the side. Importing some cut-rate jewels with questionable backgrounds and reselling them.

When they bought the house, they had done some remodeling and built a full basement under the house. An unpermitted basement that did not show on the original plans.

Only Dot and Dan knew about the basement. It was where they stored what they imported.

George moved away from the entrance and through the

empty kitchen toward the garage door. The house had a two-car garage that was completely empty, but George knew that another door led off the back mudroom and down to the basement.

A hidden door behind a small built-in bench and coat racks.

Looking George would have never known the opening was there and there was no sign around the outside of any basement.

But George knew how to open that secret door. He needed to pull on one coat hook while lifting the edge of the bench at the same time.

He started to reach for the bench and the coat hook and then stopped, realizing what he had almost done.

Dot and Dan were down there, in that basement, with all of their furniture.

His vision had told him that three men had visited Dot and Dan, forced them into the hidden basement and killed them. The men had taken all the jewels and spent seven hours that evening moving all the furniture from the home, the clothing, everything, down there, so it would look like Dot and Dan had just suddenly moved away and left the house for the bank.

The last image George had was Dot and Dan's two cars pulling out of the garage, driven by two of the killers just before dawn in March.

No one had found the hidden basement in all the bank inspections and realtor inspections.

No one ever would find that door. No one but George and the three killers even knew it was there.

George walked back toward the front door. He had no idea at all what he should do. No one would believe him if he said he had a special power that told him about the basement.

Maybe he could pretend that Dan and Dot had told him about the hidden basement, but not know how to find it, ask the realtor where it was, have the realtor find the basement and the bodies.

But that would get him answering questions he didn't have answers to. He had never really talked with Dan and Dot.

And he had no client he was looking at the house for.

He had no idea what he should do. The right thing would be to tell the realtor about the missing basement.

But that would change his life, he had no doubt.

He went back out into the growing warmth of the morning and made sure the door was locked behind him. Then he continued on with his walk.

He was back to his home, standing in his own living room, when the solution came to him.

He did some quick research, checked with construction records online, then the bank listing saying the house didn't have a basement.

And then to make sure, he checked the exact date that Dot and Dan had bought the house.

His vision had been right, just as it always had been.

They had bought the house just a few weeks after Madge died.

With shaking hands, George picked up the phone and called his old company.

Stan, the owner of the real estate firm was two years older than George and still working, often saying they would pry his cold dead fingers off the business and not a moment before. Numbers of times since Madge died Stan had offered George his position back.

George had always appreciated the gesture, but had said no. He didn't need the money and until this morning had enjoyed his daily walks and his routines.

When Stan came on the line, he was darned happy to hear from George, again offering his old job back.

"Can't do it," George said, "but got a house listing, bank owned, that just popped up on my street today. Thought it might be something you would want to latch onto so I gave it a look-see. Found some strange things. Or better put, didn't find some things. For example, I didn't find the basement."

Stan laughed. "George, you know you always had a way with houses. But sure the age isn't getting to you. Basements are the things you go down stairs to find."

George laughed. "No stairs."

"So how do you know the place is supposed to have a basement?" Stan asked.

"I started taking walks around this subdivision right after Madge died," George said. "On a number of those walks I watched the previous owners take out enough dirt through their garage in trucks to build a basement under the house."

"Okay, so they hid the stairs. And what's the problem with that?" Stan asked.

"No basement listed. Nothing permitted or recorded. Bank doesn't have it priced for a basement either. And I couldn't find any door to a basement. But if there is a basement down there, that house is a steal at the price they have on it. Might want to go give it a look."

"Damn, appreciate that," Stan said.

George smiled. Even at seventy-three, Stan never missed a good deal when it came along.

"I got a friend with some of that new equipment that he can see through walls," Stan said, "and down into the ground to find pipes and such. We'll haul that along."

"Let me know what you find," George said. "Drove me nuts not being able to find that basement door this morning."

"Sure you don't want your job back?" Stan asked.

"Only if you give me your job," George said, laughing.

Stan laughed as well, thanked him, and hung up.

George made himself stay on routine for the rest of the day, eating lunch at his normal place downtown, taking another walk around the homes in the North End of Boise along the beautiful tree-lined streets, then going home to cook himself dinner and watch television.

He went out for his normal walk the next morning at his normal time. Two police cars were in front of Dot and Dan's house and the entire yard was taped off as a crime scene.

It seemed that Dot and Dan had been found.

He stood around watching the police come in and out of the home for a few minutes, then continued on with his walk.

It was a nice morning and there was yet another house empty on Bryant Street he was waiting for a For Sale sign to go up.

That always excited him because on Bryant Street, there was just no way of knowing what a house would tell him about its owners.

Dean Wesley Smith

USA Today Bestselling Writer

Cheerleader Revelation

Sometimes to save the world, a guy must take on the cheerleaders.

BRYANT STREET

CHEERLEADER REVELATION

Sometimes, to save the world, even on Bryant Street a guy must take on the cheerleaders.

John Divine lived through a vision of the end of the world, a world ruled by cheerleaders, a world he refused to live in.

His choice obvious… He must stop them.

ONE

John Divine, leader of the chess club, scholarship student next year to MIT, and total geek, hated cheerleaders. To him they were vain, shallow, stupid, and mean-spirited. They ran in packs like wolves, preying on any unsuspecting geek stupid enough to be in their path in the hall between periods at Jericho High.

Because he didn't look like the average geek, but instead was tall with thick shoulders like his father, he had managed to avoid contact. But that didn't reduce his hate for them.

Trudi Stevens was their leader, the worst of the worst with her long blonde hair, bright white teeth, and perfect body. He often had nightmares about that body, waking up sweating and shaking with a raging hard-on. After every dream about her, he was disgusted at himself.

It didn't stop the dreams.

Then one night in October, John had a dream like no other.

It was as if a spirit had come to him in his sleep, talked to him, given him a vision of the world to come, the worst vision of ruin that John could have ever imagined. People screaming and running nude in the streets, others being helped out in clear pain, others just standing mute in shock.

It felt like the end of the world.

And all in vivid color.

In the vision, he kept thinking over and over how real it felt, that he never dreamed in color, that he didn't want to even think about the end of the world. He was going to MIT next year. The world couldn't end yet.

As John fought to get out of the vision, it slowly changed, fast-forwarded in an odd way, showing him that humanity was gone from around him.

Except Trudi.

She stood there, towering over him, surveying the ruin and tragedy around her as if she liked what she saw. She was naked, hands on her hips, nipples hard and thrusting forward.

Cold wind blew her blonde hair and she didn't seem to notice. Only the ruin seemed to please her.

Then John realized he was below her, looking up at her, seeing how she shaved her crotch, how her butt stood out a little more than he had ever noticed before, how she had a dimple on one side of one ass cheek.

All in color of course.

Then she looked down at him and smiled that damn perfect smile of hers. As she did the sky cleared, the sun came out, and everything around him suddenly cleared.

She took a deep breath that did amazing things to her chest, then motioned that he should join her on the hill, climb up to her naked body.

Right then he woke up screaming.

Or maybe shouting.

TWO

"You all right?" his dad hollered down the hall from the living room. His dad had been unemployed for six months while his mom worked at a bank. She got up early and left for work, his dad stayed up late and watched old movies.

John was their only child and just sort of stayed out of the way. He had long ago figured out that the only reason they were still together was that he hadn't gotten out of high school and left yet.

"I'm fine," he shouted back. "Just a nightmare."

His dad didn't answer, which was normal at this point.

John left his bedroom as soon as his erection was down enough to not be noticed through his pajama bottoms, and went to the bathroom down the hall in the three bedroom home. His body was shaking every step of the way as he tried desperately to get the dream out of his head.

Get the image of naked Trudi out of his mind.

Only it hadn't been a dream. He was sure of that. It had been a vision, and no matter how hard he tried, he couldn't shake the fact that what he had seen was different.

That it was real.

It was the future.

By the time he had gotten his drink of water, peed, and gone back to his room, he knew for a fact that Trudi would cause the end of the world. He was sure of that, as sure as he was about the answer to the last question on a physics test. He just didn't know how she would end the world.

Yet.

So beginning the second month of his senior year at Jericho High, John Divine set out to stop her in any way he could and save the world from all cheerleaders like her.

As with any good scientist, he knew he first had to study the problem, meaning Trudi, before finding the solution. Since any science geek in high school was basically invisible to the popular groups, he easily followed her, tracking her schedule around school.

He knew when she was in English, when she went to cheerleading practice, and what her new Volkswagen with a red flower on the door looked like. He had it all written carefully down in notebooks, just as he did his lab experiments, noting every detail because you never knew when one would matter.

Then, with his dad's camera, he took a dozen pictures of her at different places around the school and put those in the notebook as well.

But after a month it was clear to John that nothing in his preliminary study had given him any ideas on how to stop Trudi from ending everything.

Or even any idea how she might do it.

Maybe she would become a power-hungry President of the country in thirty years. She had become class president after all. Maybe she would cause a war by saying something stupid at the wrong time in the wrong place. He just didn't have any idea, yet the vision of her standing there naked haunted him every day.

He needed to take his study of her to the next level. He needed to know what she did after school, in the morning before school, and on weekends. For all he knew she was part of an alien advance force coming to take over the planet. Granted that had been done to death in movies, but that didn't make it any less possible.

He had to find out.

But taking his research to the next step posed a number of problems, not the least of which were the anti-stalking laws.

Finally he came up with a solution. From an online security sight he bought a very expensive miniature surveillance camera with short-range broadcast capability. It took a nice chunk out of his college bank account using the debit card for the purchase, but he figured that saving the world was worth it.

He boosted the camera's range to over a third of a mile and hid it on the underside of her rearview mirror in her car.

She couldn't see it. But the beauty of his positioning of the camera was that it would tell him where she was going, as well as showing her from the waist down if she were in the car. That way if someone else drove her car, he would know it.

He set up two relays, one near her house and the other near the school, to send the signal from the camera to the computer in his bedroom where he could record it.

The first three days of the new system she climbed in her car, left school, and just went home, climbing out of the car there and not using it again.

But on Friday afternoon, after cheerleader practice, he was already home and at his computer watching the feed live when she climbed into her car in the school parking lot and sat there for a minute, turned sideways as if talking to someone.

Then she did something that he knew for a fact he was going to have even more nightmares about. She raised her butt off her seat, reached under her cheerleading uniform, and pulled off her uniform pants and then her white underwear.

The vision had been right. She was so vain she shaved everywhere.

And he had an instant erection.

THREE

A man's hand and arm came across the field of vision of the camera and dove into her crotch like a mouse going for cheese after finishing a maze.

Her legs went apart and the hand played a piano solo on her key parts.

John watched as the hand moved, slowly gaining speed.

Then through the front window John saw two of the other cheerleaders come from the football field area and start toward the parking lot. It took Trudi and the extra hand a few moments longer before they saw the problem.

The hand yanked back as if scalded by a hot iron, and Trudi quickly slipped on her cheerleader pants, leaving her panties under the seat.

John had no doubt that the mouse would have a return match with the cheese after the game, but he didn't plan on watching.

Suddenly John realized he had the answer to stopping her. Those panties, tucked back under the seat, were how he could stop her.

In one of his experiments in class, and after class, he had been working on a possible chemical that would break down the molecular structure of synthetic fiber. If he could get that to work, maybe he could figure out a way to embarrass Trudi so much she would never be able to rise to a position of power enough to destroy the world.

In a few minutes Trudi drove her car home, and then thirty minutes later drove it back to school for the big game, never getting her white panties from under the seat.

The moment she parked her car in the school lot and got out, John headed for the front room to ask his dad if he could borrow the car for a few minutes. He told his dad he needed it to go back to school for a homework assignment he had left there.

"Figures," his dad said, shaking his head while downing a beer. "Friday night and you're doing homework."

"A kid as good-looking as you are should get out of the books once in a while," his mother said.

"I know," John said, ignoring the conversation that had gone on for years now.

"Dinner's in forty minutes," his mother said, handing him the keys.

"I won't be that long," John said, and dashed for the car.

Twenty minutes later he was home with Trudi's underwear stuffed in his pocket.

The next Monday he was back in the chemistry lab doing experiments on a tiny patch of cloth cut from near the seat area of the panties.

Things after that settled into a routine for a few months. He studied her movements, watched the hand grab for cheese a number of times, and worked in the lab. As far as his professor was concerned, he was working on a way to make the molecular bonds in clothing stronger, to make clothes last longer. His professor followed his progress closely, astounded that he could do the work he was doing.

It was in January, on a late evening session in the lab, that he finally hit on the chemical compound he had been looking for. It was colorless, and easily contained by glass.

The beauty of his find was that when one diluted drop was put against a piece of the cloth, nothing happened.

But when a certain frequency of sound was directed at the treated cloth, the cloth broke apart and completely vanished in less than thirty seconds.

John could barely contain himself he was so excited. Even his mom noticed at dinner and asked him why he was so happy suddenly. He'd told her a good grade in a tough class and she nodded and patted him on the shoulder. His dad had only shaken his head.

John knew he was a disappointment to his father. His dad had wanted a jock, a football player with a mouse hand. Instead he'd gotten a geek kid with a computer and a desire to save the world. Maybe someday John would make him proud.

Or at least make him rich.

FOUR

For the next two weeks John repeated his experiment in private, making sure it actually worked the way he wanted it to. His teacher thought he was still stuck and hadn't made a breakthrough. John figured there was no point in having any way to trace what was going to happen to Trudi back to him.

After that he worked on his plan to really embarrass her, and end all chance of her causing the end of the world.

First he studied Trudi's home, thinking he might get his "Cloth Away" as he was calling it, into her laundry room, but soon tossed that idea out. Her parents were security freaks and her mom was always home. No chance of getting his new chemical in there.

So instead he studied the city's water supply and discovered that it would be easy to get his harmless, tasteless, odorless chemical into it. Even with the higher security these days, only one old guard sat in a truck near the fenced off lake. John could come down out of the trees on the other side of the lake, duck under the fence and simply put his chemical into the water.

He spent a week doing the calculations on how much he would need, then another week making the ten gallons of Cloth Away.

Then he studied the city's water supply, calculating how long it would take for the water with Cloth Away in it to get through the system and to Trudi's home. Then adding three extra days to give her time to do some laundry, he figured out the exact night and went up to the inlet area of the supply from the lake and casually dumped his stuff into the water.

Seven days later, much to the pleasant surprise of his father, he went to a basketball game, making sure to wear only clothing that hadn't been washed in the last few days.

He sat just off to the edge of the student section, and got there early enough that he was only one seat off the floor level.

Trudi and the other cheerleaders led the students in a few yells as they arrived, but mostly just huddled off to one side and talked and laughed, sometimes staring at the basketball players.

John tried not to stare at her, tried not to let the vision of the end of the world fade from his thoughts.

Around him the stands had filled. They were playing a team from sixty miles away, and most of the fans across the court were from there. That was good, because the frequency of sound he needed to make Trudi's uniform drop away would be hard to exactly control.

Finally, John could wait no longer. Trudi had been bouncing up and down along the sidelines during every timeout, and as the coach again called one, the cheerleaders took the court.

John eased the battery-powered horn out of his pocket, and with a deep breath, clicked it on, sending the silent ultrasonic sound across the court at the bouncing cheer-leaders.

At the woman who would end the world.

Suddenly it became clear that he had miscalculated a little with the intensity of the sound from the horn.

The cheerleaders uniforms all sort of crumbled, dropped to the floor, and vanished, leaving the stunned girls screaming and covering themselves.

Around him John heard others shouting and screaming

as the ultra-sonic sound from his horn bounced off the walls of the gym and came back and hit everyone in the home team stands.

Amazing how many people had done laundry in the last few days.

John instantly turned off the horn and hid it in his jacket, but the damage was done.

The very overweight woman sitting beside him lost her dress and underwear. Just about everyone in the stands around and behind him found themselves suddenly and completely nude.

People of all ages and sizes.

It was not a pretty sight.

Panic set in as people shouted and screamed and tried to cover themselves and run for the doors at the same time.

The visiting team and fans just stared in shock as even the home team basketball uniforms vanished.

John was pushed hard from behind and tumbled head-over-heels onto the gym floor, banging his elbow and head. He just lay there, on his back, eyes closed, trying not to think about what he had done.

A couple people accidentally kicked him with their bare feet in the stampede for the doors.

He never opened his eyes. It would have been too painful to watch the damage. It hadn't been Trudi that had ended the world, it had been him and his horn.

Finally the screaming and panic were over, ending almost as quickly as it had come, leaving only a low level of talking and uncomfortable laughing of the visiting team.

He finally got the courage to open his eyes.

People were still moving in all directions and Trudi was standing over him, completely nude and not seeming to care.

It was the same image as in his vision.

Around them the game, the world of high school Friday night basketball had ended

And just like in his vision, there she stood.

She bent down and extended him a hand to help him to his feet. "You all right, John?"

"I think-think so," he said, stunned that she knew his name.

"Good," she said, nodding. "You took a nasty fall there."

He rubbed the back of his head and laughed. "Yeah, I did. But I'll live."

Then he realized he was talking to Trudi, the woman he hated, the woman who he had thought was going to end the world in his vision. And she was nude, just as his vision had said she would be.

He quickly slipped off his coat and helped her put it on. The coat was long enough to cover just about everything.

"No point in getting too cold," he said.

She laughed as around them dozens and dozens of the remaining nude people who hadn't stampeded into the cold winter night were slowly getting covered back up by helpful people.

"Thanks," she said, zipping up the coat to make sure everything stayed covered. Then she felt the large horn and battery pack in the front pocket of the coat.

"What's this?' she asked, squeezing the hard horn from the outside of the coat and winking at him. "You happy to see me or something?"

"Always," he said, smiling at her.

"I know," she said, "considering you followed me around school for a month and then put a camera in my car."

In all his life John had never been so surprised, so shocked. How could she have known? He glanced around the basketball court where a hundred people still milled trying to figure out what to do next.

All he wanted was to run and run hard, maybe leave town. Maybe leave the country.

Why hadn't she reported him? Did she know that he had watched her and the football player's mouse hand? He could feel his face turning red.

"How did I know?" she asked, laughing at what must have been a shocked look on his face. "You're not the only one who's going to MIT next year, you know."

Now he was *really* shocked.

Trudi at MIT? She was a cheerleader. He hadn't heard she had gotten into MIT. He hadn't even given it a thought. How closed minded had he been?

The answer to that question was easy: *Very.*

"What I want to know," she said, holding onto his arm clearly to make sure he didn't run, "is how you managed all this?"

"Chemical breakdown of molecules," he said, "triggered by sound."

She patted the horn in the pocket of the coat she was wearing. "Brilliant. And you put the chemical into the city water supply, right?"

He nodded.

"Brilliant again," she said.

Then she laughed the most beautiful laugh he had ever heard. "Don't worry, your secret is safe with me. I haven't had this much fun in a long, long time."

"Thanks," he said, looking into her blue eyes and realizing that there really was a depth in there, a person with a real brain and a real sense of humor. "But to be honest it worked a little better than I had hoped."

"Only aiming at the cheerleaders, huh?"

She looked at him, smiling.

"Of course," he said, his tension of her knowing what he had done easing. "Actually, you more than the others?"

"Wanted to embarrass me, huh?"

"That, and see you naked," he said, finally admitting to himself the real drive behind his idea, planted by his vision.

"Well?"

"Well what?" he asked.

"Well what did you think of me naked?"

"Perfect," he said, smiling at her. "Worth every minute of the end of the world."

"Seems to me the world is just beginning," she said, smiling up at him. "How about you walk me to my car and drive me home to get some clothes? Then over a pizza that you're going to buy me I want to hear every detail of this crazy idea."

"And then?" he asked, smiling at her.

"Then," she said, taking his arm and turning him toward the gym door, "if you're a really good boy, I'll let you blow your horn again."

"I like that idea a lot," he said, smiling back at her.

The end of the world had never sounded so good.

BRYANT STREET

USA Today Bestselling Writer

DEAN WESLEY

SMITH

A Story of Conforming...

BRYANT STREET

BRYANT STREET

I fear Bryant Street more than anything on the planet. Honestly, when in a standard subdivision, I always get lost, turned around, and slightly panicked. Not kidding.

In a writer's workshop in 1982, I was challenged to write a story with the first line "The Wolves Were Howling on Bryant Street." I knew instantly what the wolves represented. As a fiction writer, doing battle with the wolves never ends.

This is the story that started it all.

ONE

The wolves were howling on Bryant Street.

Duncan nudged the orange slice closer to the edge of his plate of ham and eggs and tried not to listen. He forced himself to concentrate on the loud clanking of pans in the kitchen of the Denny's Restaurant, then the loud, constant chatter of the large-thighed waitress.

It did no good.

He could still hear the wolves.

The waitress had started it all. She'd asked him why he never ate the orange slice that came with his late-night breakfast. She'd said most of her regular customers ate it, why didn't he?

Simple. He hated fruit with ham and eggs. Just the thought made the grease curl up into a ball in his stomach. But for some reason, every restaurant had an orange slice with ham and eggs. Stupid custom.

He had been about to tell the waitress, in so many plain words, that it was his business what he did with his orange slice when the wolves started to howl.

The wolves of Bryant Street.

Bryant Street was after Duncan.

He flipped the orange slice over and thought back to the first and only time he had been on Bryant Street. It had been a warm Friday afternoon two months ago, shortly after he graduated from college with his degree in electrical engineering. Road construction blocked the main street past the mall and he had been forced to turn his VW Bug onto Bryant Street.

Right away he had known he was in trouble.

The perfect houses all looked the same.

Each had lots of shrubs outside, two bedrooms inside, and an attached room for two cars.

The further down the street he got, the more uncomfortable he felt, like he was listening to the music in Jaws before seeing the shark.

He glanced first left, then right.

Perfectly spaced trees planted exactly correct distances apart fought to hypnotize him with their monotone swaying.

The green shutters on all the houses closed in around him and the evenly cut lawns beckoned to him like a soft bed to a man without sleep. He gasped for each breath.

On both sides front doors opened, ready and willing to swallow him.

The smooth driveways sucked at his little car.

Sweat dripped into his eyes as he fought to keep the Bug in the middle of the road.

He glanced back.

He'd only gone a hundred trees.

Five more trees and he couldn't take it any more.

He gunned his Bug into a u-turn between two Pintos.

Bryant Street now seemed to stretch for miles down a dark, forbidding tunnel of jagged branches.

He jammed the gas pedal to the floor, his mind racing with the fear of a flat.

Or engine trouble.

The trees slashed at him.

The street rolled, pitched the car from side to side.

He fought his way down the road tree by tree, the entire time keeping his gaze locked on the faint light ahead.

Finally, after what seemed to be all afternoon, he

reached the detour, ducked between a Caddy and a Datsun, and headed back downtown.

He had never gone near Bryant Street again.

Now, it was coming for him, sending the wolves to round him up like so much mutton.

Damn it all, anyway. It wouldn't get him without a fight.

"Mister? You all right?" the waitress asked, popping her gum.

Duncan shook himself and looked up at her. He must have looked a little funny, sitting there, leaning away from the window. The wolves were still howling.

"Can you hear them?" Duncan asked.

"Yeah. They're awful, aren't they?" The whine in her voice reminded Duncan of a smoke detector going off. "Someday they're going to get a good band in that bar and fill the place. I keep telling Craig—he's the boss—that if he would just—"

"No," Duncan said. "Not the band. The wolves. The wolves from Bryant Street. Listen. Don't you hear them?"

She popped her gum once more. "Can't say as I do." She flipped his ticket upside down near his plate and walked away.

He should have known she wouldn't hear them. The street wanted him. He'd have to fight his own battle.

He picked up the orange slice and ate it quickly. He'd give them this first battle, but nothing more.

The wolves quit howling.

He finished his eggs, but left the ham. His stomach was

upset enough without putting ham on top of an orange slice.

TWO

From that night on, the fight with the wolves from Bryant Street became intense.

Every time Duncan got one step out of line, Wham-o, howl-time. And each time the wolves got louder and louder. It drove him crazy. It got to the point he felt they could hear his every thought.

For example, one month after the wolves started howling, on a Wednesday night, he had a date with Constance, a tall blonde with a high laugh and large features.

Constance was the lady who cut his hair while rubbing her large features against his back and arms. He loved the way her fingers massaged his scalp and had dreams of her massaging other places, including her large features.

By eight in the evening they had stormed and occupied a dark, lower booth in a plush hotel bar. One of those places where the backs of the booths were planters and the seats a form of fake leather.

They were getting down to the point of being real cozy, when suddenly, an old woman in the booth behind them looked through the plants and then whispered to her toothless old man, "Is that Constance's husband?"

Duncan turned around slowly, pushed one large bunch of plant leaves aside so he could see the shocked look on the old woman's face, and then looked the old bag right in her gray eyes. "Of course I'm not. What fun would that be?"

The wolves started howling their thing.

Duncan could hear them right over the music and the gasps of shock and indignation from the old woman. The wolves' howls were long and drawn out and sounded plain vicious. He imagined saliva dripping from their teeth as they threw back their heads and ruined his evening.

And, for the first time, they sounded close.

Almost right outside.

By this point he knew better than to ask anyone if they heard them. "Look," he said to Constance. "I just remembered that I have this appointment. You understand. Maybe another time, huh?"

With one last longing look at those large features, he stood.

Damn it all. He loved those fingers.

He'd fix those wolves for this.

He patted her hand like a father consoling a child, moved his scotch with reverence to the center of the table, and headed for the door of the bar. He had packed his father's deer rifle in the trunk of his car. He was going to bag himself a wolf tonight.

The wolves weren't in the parking lot or anywhere else around the side of the hotel. But the level of their howls never diminished. It was as if he were surrounded.

They didn't stop howling until the police arrested him for scaring hotel guests by stomping through the flowerbeds outside their rooms with a rifle.

THREE

With the wolves hounding him, life became one big bore.

Time after time they stopped him from one activity or another. He always looked for them without luck. Each time they sounded close, but somehow he knew they were still over on Bryant Street. And no way was he going back there.

No sir.

No way.

After a while he tried to convince himself he was making them up. Didn't work.

Their howls froze him, made him stop whatever he was doing. They were too real sounding.

But there were a few things in Duncan's life the wolves didn't seem to mind. One was his work with a small company downtown. They also didn't seem to mind baseball or Debbie.

Debbie was short and cute in a plain sort of way. She had shoulder length brown hair, perfect teeth, and tiny feet. She was also a complete take-her-home-to-meet-mother prude.

He had met Debbie the week before the wolves started their terrorist action. She worked in a downtown department store in the small-appliance section. He had gone in for a new toaster. The night before, while drunk, he had used his old one for a football. He had thought he was Joe Willy and threw a perfect pass through the window while fading back behind the blocking of his couch.

For the first month, Duncan wasn't sure why he kept asking Debbie out. Possibly for the challenge. He figured she finally agreed for the same reason.

That and the fact the he had what she called "big potential."

After the war started with the wolves, dates with Debbie were the only peaceful ones he had. For a while he suspected it was something she or her rich father was doing. But after searching a hundred places for speakers, he gave up trying to figure out how.

Dates with Debbie were boring, plain and simple. The same kind he'd had back in high school: movies, hamburgers or dinner, and a lot of talk about everything but the real subject on his mind. Every night, after he dropped her off, he went downtown and got drunk. The wolves didn't seem to mind that much either, as long as he kept his hands to himself.

One night, after six months of dating Debbie and fighting the wolves by alternately running from them or searching for them, the battle shifted.

For some unremembered reason, Duncan had promised Debbie to take her dancing. Debbie was having so much fun, she even had a few drinks. It must have been the drinks, because they started dancing all the slow dances and Debbie kept getting closer and closer.

By halfway through the night she was rubbing up and down and up and down real slow like she was carefully sanding a fine antique. It drove him crazy.

He kept waiting for the wolves to start their howl, but they didn't.

Later, after he was rubbed raw, they ended up at his apartment. That was the first time he had talked her into going up there.

She'd had four strawberry daiquiris and looked dazed. She didn't say a word about the three flights of stairs, but her face looked pale by the time she got inside.

"Bathroom's there," he pointed.

"Nice place," she lied, and headed for the door he had indicated.

He went into the kitchen and poured them both another drink of scotch. He didn't even know if she liked scotch or not, but it didn't matter. He used his best Goodwill glasses and only put one ice cube in hers so it wouldn't be too watered down when he drank it later.

He'd only taken a sip when the toilet flushed and she came out. She staggered straight up to him, pulled his head down, and kissed him with strawberry breath.

He set his scotch down quickly as she started hoeing his mouth with her tongue, planting strawberry seeds with drunken skill.

Fifteen minutes later they had worked their way to the bedroom and removed all their clothes.

"Careful," she said when they started.

He said, "Yeah," and she rubbed and he rubbed and the pace picked quickly up.

Then the wolves started howling.

Major battle time.

Tonight they sounded loud, closer, and extra mean, but there was no way he was going to stop. It was about time he learned to ignore them.

"I love it," Debbie said softly as she twisted her head from side to side. She started rubbing faster and faster. "I love it... I love it... I love you..."

He noticed the word change, but didn't stop.

Nothing was going to make him stop.

No word, no howl, nothing.

Debbie kept saying she loved him and the wolves kept howling and Duncan did his best just to keep up.

Finally, the situation was to that critical time which marked the boundary between thinking, "Why not?" and wondering "Why?" when the wolves stopped howling.

This time the silence made him pause.

"Oh, don't stop," Debbie said. "You feel so good."

A low growl came from near the door.

He tried to ignore it and go on with Debbie's request when a second mean-sounding growl stopped him in mid-rub.

He glanced around.

The wolves were no longer howling from Bryant Street. The battle had moved into his own bedroom where they now circled his bed.

On the left, two were crouched, ready to spring.

Another stood, hair on its back on end, growling. Saliva dripped from its yellow teeth and formed a wet spot on the rug.

He turned to the right. Two more were there.

He was dead for sure. He closed his eyes and waited for the first rip of his flesh. He was going to die in the missionary position without a fight.

What a way to go.

"Duncan, dear. Are you all right?"

"I don't know," he said and opened his eyes. There couldn't really be wolves in his bedroom. Why didn't Debbie see them?

How could they harm him and not her?

Made no sense.

He must be imagining things. That was it. If he ignored them, they would go away.

"Don't stop," Debbie said, her voice almost pleading. She started to move again and without thinking, he did too.

Out of the corner of his eye he saw the largest wolf take a step toward the bed and crouch to spring.

Duncan stopped again, bare essentials cruelly exposed to the pack.

The wolf stopped.

Standoff. Duncan looked both ways. They had all moved closer.

What the hell did they want? He'd been nice to Debbie. This had been mostly her idea. He didn't know what they wanted him to do.

He looked into the pale blue eyes of the largest wolf. It growled real low and angry-like.

Suddenly, what it wanted was clear to Duncan.

He glanced down at Debbie. She was watching him with

a look of concern. The wolves wanted him to tell her that he loved her. He might be able to do that.

Maybe.

She was a nice girl. He sort of liked her. Telling her he loved her was the right thing to do and the wolves always left him alone when he did the right thing.

"Debbie," he said, "I... I..."

He turned back to the largest wolf hoping for one last chance. The wolf bared its teeth and growled.

"Debbie, I love you," he quickly said. That should do it.

It damn well better.

Debbie pulled him down into a hard hug that pressed his ear into her right breast. "Really, Duncan? Do you mean it?"

She kissed him with her mouth open and her orthodontist teeth showing. Then, without hesitation, she started to move again. He didn't know if he should join her.

The wolves were still there.

But his body won. He couldn't help himself and he slowly joined her rhythm.

Two of the wolves snarled again and the largest wolf stuck its cold nose against the side of his leg.

He jerked and rolled away from the wolf, pulling Debbie over on top of him.

"Oh, Duncan. You're so much fun."

She pulled her legs up under her and started practicing her belly dancing moves on his stomach. She was a fine belly dancer, he quickly discovered.

He lay there and looked from side to side at the wolves.

He hadn't imagined that cold nose. The wolves might be invisible to everyone else, but they were real enough to his touch.

And they still weren't happy with him.

They were in close all the way around the bed. He could smell their stale breath. He had to do something and do it quick.

The biggest wolf again touched him with its cold nose.

Duncan jumped and Debbie gave a little squeal of joy.

"Debbie! Stop!"

Debbie pulled her hair away from her face and looked down at him. Her cheeks were flushed and she had this hungry look in her eyes.

The same look the wolves had.

"I need to ask you something." He checked the wolves on his right and then on his left. He could imagine his bloodstains on their yellowed teeth. They weren't giving him a chance.

They had him surrounded.

They had won this battle and the war.

"Debbie," he said as softly as he could, his mind racing for any other way. Anything. But this was what the wolves wanted. They had him naked, flat on his back, unarmed.

"Debbie, would you marry me?"

"What?"

The wolves all took a few steps backwards. It worked. He couldn't believe it.

"What did you say?" Debbie asked.

"Oh, nothing," Duncan said. The wolves started toward the bed again, all growling.

"Would you marry me?"

"Do you really mean it?" Debbie asked. "You know I've loved you since the first day we met."

"Would I have asked if I didn't?"

Damn the wolves anyway.

She kissed him hard and again started to rub, already trying to polish his rough edges.

He glanced around. Only the largest wolf remained. It curled up and went promptly to sleep in the corner.

After a short time, Duncan started rubbing back.

They were married seven months later in a big church wedding. He was the perfect groom.

Everyone said so.

They moved into a house her daddy bought for them on Bryant Street and he went to work for her daddy's corporation.

People only thought it just a little odd that he built a dog run in their back yard, even though it matched all the other dog runs on Bryant Street.

They don't have a dog.

No one on Bryant Street has a dog.

NEWSLETTER SIGN-UP

Follow Dean on BookBub

Be the first to know!
Just sign up for the Dean Wesley Smith newsletter, and keep up with the latest news, releases and so much more—even the occasional giveaway.

So, what are you waiting for? To sign up go to deanwesleysmith.com.

But wait! There's more. Sign up for the WMG Publishing newsletter, too, and get the latest news and releases from all of the WMG authors and lines, including Kristine Kathryn Rusch, Kristine Grayson, Kris Nelscott, *Pulphouse Fiction Magazine, Smith's Monthly,* and so much more.
To sign up go to wmgpublishing.com.

ABOUT THE AUTHOR

DEAN WESLEY SMITH

Considered one of the most prolific writers working in modern fiction, with more than 30 million books sold, *USA Today* bestselling writer Dean Wesley Smith published far more than a hundred novels in forty years, and hundreds of short stories across many genres.

At the moment he produces novels in several major series, including the time travel Thunder Mountain novels set in the Old West, the galaxy-spanning Seeders Universe series, the urban fantasy Ghost of a Chance series, a superhero series starring Poker Boy, and a mystery series featuring the retired detectives of the Cold Poker Gang.

His monthly magazine, *Smith's Monthly*, which consists of only his own fiction, premiered in October 2013 and offers readers more than 70,000 words per issue, including a new and original novel every month.

During his career, Dean also wrote a couple dozen *Star Trek* novels, the only two original *Men in Black* novels, Spider-Man and X-Men novels, plus novels set in gaming and television worlds. Writing with his wife Kristine Kathryn Rusch under the name Kathryn Wesley, he wrote the novel for the NBC miniseries The Tenth Kingdom and other books for *Hallmark Hall of Fame* movies.

He wrote novels under dozens of pen names in the worlds of comic books and movies, including novelizations of almost a dozen films, from *The Final Fantasy* to *Steel* to *Rundown.*

Dean also worked as a fiction editor off and on, starting at Pulphouse Publishing, then at *VB Tech Journal,* then Pocket Books, and now at WMG Publishing, where he and Kristine Kathryn Rusch serve as series editors for the acclaimed *Fiction River* anthology series.

For more information about Dean's books and ongoing projects, please visit his website at www.deanwesley-smith.com and sign up for his newsletter.

For more information:

www.deanwesleysmith.com

facebook.com/deanwsmith3

patreon.com/deanwesleysmith

BB bookbub.com/authors/dean-wesley-smith

EXPANDED COPYRIGHT INFORMATION

Published by WMG Publishing